About the Author

I am Noel Taylor and I am an inventor, singer-songwriter, artist, author and broadcaster.

One To Free

To Catheryn Thompson
happy haloween.

Noel Taylor

One To Free

Olympia Publishers
London

www.olympiapublishers.com
OLYMPIA PAPERBACK EDITION

Copyright © Noel Taylor 2023

The right of Noel Taylor to be identified as author of
this work has been asserted in accordance with sections 77 and 78 of
the Copyright, Designs and Patents Act 1988.

All Rights Reserved

No reproduction, copy or transmission of this publication
may be made without written permission.
No paragraph of this publication may be reproduced,
copied or transmitted save with the written permission of the publisher,
or in accordance with the provisions
of the Copyright Act 1956 (as amended).

Any person who commits any unauthorised act in relation to
this publication may be liable to criminal
prosecution and civil claims for damage.

A CIP catalogue record for this title is
available from the British Library.

ISBN: 978-1-80074-949-8

This is a work of fiction.
Names, characters, places and incidents originate from the writer's
imagination. Any resemblance to actual persons, living or dead, is
purely coincidental.

First Published in 2023

Olympia Publishers
Tallis House
2 Tallis Street
London
EC4Y 0AB
Printed in Great Britain

Dedication

This book I dedicate to my parents who passed away into a better life.

Chapter 1

The rain heaped upon Rodney as he quickened his stealthy steps. His only thought was to find shelter — and fast. The torrent became immense. He just pounced into the nearest shop going.

It was a book shop. He immediately became bedazzled by the selection on offer. Like a youngster in a candy shop he began looking. Through encyclopaedias at first. He fleetingly gazed at the assistant, only noticing that she had blonde hair and a pretty face. Unusual for Rodney as he was a full-bodied, full-blooded male, without question. He pondered further. He looked at book upon book for at least twenty minutes. Another customer came in, making two in all. Blast, he thought to himself, there go my chances of chatting up that broad alone. If only I hadn't been so interested in the books.

Rodney perused a book by Anthea Turner for quite a while as he fingered his unkempt hair, caused by the rain. He strolled past the middle of the shop, where fiction was on display, as he was disinterested in anything that was not fact. He got his comb out and gave his wavey hair a quick run through, thinking to himself that with his hair still wet, he will save himself a fortune on hair gel. He procrastinated more and more. Then he fixed his eyes on the *Holy Bible*. This can't be so bad, he thought, after all it is the best-selling book in the world. He liked the colourful cover. Rodney uncarefully clasped it and the book dropped to the floor. It opened at the section called Luke, Chapter 10, verse 18.

He read the words out loud, "He replied, I saw Satan fall like lightning from Heaven." Suddenly, the shop was ablaze with fire. All hell broke loose, literally.

The assistant grabbed for the fire extinguisher. It ignited and exploded with ferocious velocity. The poor girl had no chance. Rodney and the other customer looked at each other through the flames and smoke. Suddenly, the man was totally consumed. The fire was so intense that his body was charred before he hit the ground. Rodney instinctively reached down to pick up the *Holy Bible* in amongst the fire. Even though he was not given to religious beliefs, he felt no pain as he clenched it tightly.

He ran to the door, opened it and raced into the torrential rain. The Bible, he noted, was intact. Rodney's only thought was to get as far away from the shop as quickly as possible.

Not knowing why, he ran almost blindly into the wind, with rain directed at his eyes, towards a church that he had seen on numerous journeys in this familiar town, Royal Leamington Spa. He raced in. Luckily, it was a Sunday morning and the remnants of the congregation were dispersing.

Immediately he waltzed up to the Pastor, hoping to appear cool, calm and collected, when really he had the swan thing where his outward appearance was no giveaway. 'Please, vicar, can I speak with you in private?'

The priest obliged. 'Yes of course,' he replied. The canon made his apologies to the two people he was conversing with.

The two people noticed that something was wrong. Rodney was sweating profusely. They wandered away, occasionally glancing back. Rodney was in no mood for waiting around. His panic-stricken state was obvious to the verger as they silently walked into the palatial church wing.

The priest had a lot of things to do, although he never let on throughout their conversation. 'Please sit down, sir,' the mild voiced canon said.

'Please vicar, you must help me.' The young man reiterated all that had just happened. The canon realised that from the fumbling and stuttering that Rodney was in no fit state to be left alone. The story was given in record time.

'The police must be informed of this,' said the middle-aged Pastor who was balding badly. 'You came to the right place first though,' said the excited priest. Inwardly, he was hoping to add another member to his flock. Sounds like another born-again Christian has come to Christ, he thought. The Pastor was also sweating by now. The perspiration was dribbling off the vicar's large nose. 'The thing that I am worried about is are the police going to believe this?' the vicar unthinkingly blurted out.

This worried Rodney a lot. Rodney was normally a cool dude. Aged thirty-nine, he thought that he had experienced everything that life had to throw at him. This was all new to him. His mind was working overtime. The priest was babbling away, but he was oblivious. What are you going to do now, Rodders? He was thinking and thinking again. Run away to Ireland was one of the first thoughts that came to him.

'Jesus,' the priest said and for some reason that word stuck in Rodney's mind. The canon kept on and on. All Rodney could think was how he could get out of this? He had to get away. The poor priest was talking calmly and coherently, but Rodney wasn't listening.

'May I get you a coffee? Perhaps you would like some tea? I find tea calms one down,' said the Eton-educated man.

There was absolutely no reply from the frustrated man. The canon repeated the words again. Still no response. By now, the vicar realised that this man was having a nervous breakdown. His name was Burt Stries, and with a plethora of titles, beckoned the young assistant pastor through the glass doors, in from the other room.

A young, frail looking, but smartly dressed and good looking by anyone's standards, priest walked in majestically, cool as you like.

'How can I help?' asked the young man.

Suddenly, the open door was an escape from all that had just occurred. Rodney leapt out of the room, brushing past the rector in an alien (to him) manner. Burt could do nothing, his hands were tied. He didn't want Rodney to get into trouble and he did not want him to go to a psychiatric hospital where they would treat him as if he was mad.

Rodney legged it as fast as he could up the parade, an area of Leamington that is full of shops. Being a Sunday, it was bereft of folk, which was probably why the man slowed to a peaceful pace. Rodney liked it quiet at the best of times. His attention was caught by a salubrious shop front. It was nearing Christmas time and he suddenly noted that Christmas begins with the word Christ. It hit him hard. He thought to himself, am I becoming religious? I haven't given God a second thought. Why this? Why me, why now? Rodney pondered, all of my life I haven't been too bad I suppose. Have I just been saved from certain death? The bookshop was a positive furnace. How come I am still here? Rodney took two steps into the doorway and peered around to see that no one was looking. He clasped his hands together and quickly said, 'Thank you, God.' His next step was to go to the cafe which was nearly adjacent to the Christmas adorned shop. He kept thinking to himself, calm down, Rodders, calm down. He strolled into the relatively decent establishment. Not many people about, he mused.

A rather unpleasant looking bloke said, 'What do you want?' Rodney was not impressed by his brashness and the appearance of the man. He noted his eyes. Rodney always knew that bad eye contact meant that the person was unfriendly or suspicious of him. He also clocked his unshaven face. Shall I just ignore the chap and vacate the cafe, or do I put up with this? He noticed how cosily warm it was and opted for the latter.

'I'll have a cup of tea, please.' He thought to himself that the flapjack looked just the job, but then he changed his mind. Normally Rodney had a distinct liking for the treat, but for some unknown reason, this usually rather impulsive man didn't do his usual act. A little of what you fancy does you good, was his motto.

'Eighty pence,' said the decidedly uncouth guy.

'Thanks,' replied Rodney, wishing to get away from the young man. No reply was forthcoming from him. Rodney found a seat near to the window. I am a nosy bleeder, he told himself. He peered out. Cars were always one of his favourite topics. A Peugeot 406 cabriolet cruised by.

Rodney's heart almost skipped a beat. His favourite car in the whole wide world had just passed before his eyes. This little incident cheered Rodney up no end. He glanced round to view two very friendly girls. They were both sixteen. They are about my age. He laughed to himself, knowing full well that he was old enough to be their father. This didn't perturb him. He smiled an awkward smile at them. He was normally nervous of women. They looked simultaneously at him and giggled. There were smiles all round. I could be in here, he pondered. He felt radiant and confident. Girls like a giggle, he thought. But nothing witty came to mind. I know, I will ask their names. Then he thought of his dear wife back home in Coventry. I should get back home to

Sharon soon. But hey, she knows what I'm like, always making women laugh, always trying to make everyone laugh. But for some unknown reason, his wit had dried up so he left it. He gingerly sipped his tea. Damn, no sugar. He frowned mildly as he concentrated on the task at hand. He perused the outside. It was still raining, but nothing major. His thoughts went to his wife again. She's good to me, she trusts me oodles. What will she make of the fire? Will she believe me? Will anybody out there believe me? The priest seemed to believe me, or did he? What was he saying? I should have listened to the man. He glanced at the girls. Again they giggled and good eye contact was made by them.

'What are your names?' Rodney asked.

'Charlotte,' said one excitedly.

The other one wasn't keen at all. She forced out a, 'Debbie'.

'I am Rodney,' he asserted.

Charlotte analysed Rodney in great detail. She noted his long neck, dark brown eyes, black hair and tiny ears. She thought that his eyebrows meeting in the middle was a bad sign, remembering what her mother used to say — where eyebrows meet there lies deceit. As Charlotte inspected Rodney's features, she became aroused by his good looks and had a hot flush.

'Where are you from then young man?' this teenager cheekily said.

'I'm from Coventry,' he replied. 'Where are you from?' he said inquisitively.

'We're from up the road, London,' she joked.

Rodney forced a laugh. His mind wandered to what his next move was. I had better think of a way out of this. The police are sure to be looking for a culprit.

The girls noted Rodney's lack of a quick response. They

finished their coffee and walked slowly out of the cafe. Charlotte and Debbie both said a polite goodbye to him, Debbie mentioning to her companion that Rodney looked troubled, as they stepped onto the pavement. He belatedly said cheerio, as his mind was elsewhere. Troubled being the operative word. He became overtly nervous. He decided to walk a while. I'll leave the car a while, he mused. Walking always calmed Rodney down somewhat. He exited the shop rather fast. Perhaps I should have had some food, he pondered. He wandered down the parade and thought to himself how nice the shop fronts looked. He paused at a pet shop frontage. Nice Labrador puppies and a nice price too. I could do with a golden retriever. My son would adore it. Maybe he could have it for Christmas. Rodney was always the kind-hearted soul. Never tight. He walked on thinking how four hundred and twenty pounds wasn't exactly breaking the bank. He made greater strides as he fought through the street. The pub, he thought, I will go into a quiet pub. A pie and a pint was what Rodney decided to get. A steak and kidney pie in fact.

He sipped the lager tentatively. It went down faster than he expected and soon one became ten. Now what am I going to do? I can't drive. But Rodney was not in any mood for logical thinking. He was on the road to ruin. I know, I'll get myself to the nearest hotel.

He left the public house with ease as it goes, considering the quantity of alcohol consumed. It was seven o'clock and his slight stagger was noticed by many people. He heard the bad sound of a karaoke in progress and made straight for the door of the establishment. Luckily, by sheer fluke, it was a hotel. Rodney went straight to the reception to book in first. He sunk into the carpet of the posh place. He waited as the skeleton crew dealt with other customers. He gazed at the crystal chandeliered ceiling with its elaborate artwork surround. He surveyed the massive rooms from the foyer. Nice women, he noted and this geezer on the microphone isn't half bad. Something by Barry White, ah that's it, 'My first, my last, my everything.'

'Can I help you, sir?' came the nice sounding voice from behind him. Rodney turned to a glamorous lady with long, flowing brown hair, prominent eyes and analytical eyes. She oozed confidence. She said, rather aloofly, 'Can I get you a room, sir?'

'Yes, you can thank you.' Rodney was aware of the fact that he had been drinking rather heavily and tried not to get too close to the girl.

'I only have a double room,' she lied, having been told to sell off the big rooms first by her manager.

'Yes, that will be fine,' said Rodney, never one to fuss on the price.

'That will be fifty-two pounds.'

He grinned broadly as he fumbled for his wallet. A large wad was revealed to the receptionist. Rodney always kept plenty of money on him as this gave him oodles of confidence. He panicked mildly as he fought to remember the cost the lady had said. Ah ha, that's it Rodders, fifty-two pounds. He produced three twenty-pound notes and toyed with the idea of telling her to keep the change. But then he remembered how his finances were out of sync.

'Thank you,' said the appreciative woman.

Rodney stared at her pert bottom in the long, flowing dress that she had somehow managed to slip into. 'Have you any bags, sir?' she asked politely.

'No.'

'Okay sir, there's your card. You have room thirteen, a very nice room.' With that she banged the bell on the counter with thunderous force. 'And there is your change.'

A rotund man swaggered awkwardly up to the counter.

'Thanks,' said Rodney to the lady and looked at the porter as if killing two birds with one stone. Rodney was familiar with the upper echelons of life. He had worked in a hotel in the distant past and knew the score. However, he was no toff and was always friendly to porters and the like. 'Has the room got en suite bathroom?' Rodney slurred slightly.

'I haven't a clue, sir.'

Both men were silent throughout the smooth ride of the lift which had mirrors all over, except the floor.

'Staying here long?' asked the porter.

'Just the one night,' said Rodney, slurring all the more.

It was obvious to everyone that night that he was totally sloshed, especially when he sang 'New York, New York'.

Another five pints were drunk with consummate ease that night. He saw the final act at the karaoke and then staggered to his room. He slid the card that he had been given across the door panel. Nothing! He tried again. Still nothing! Oops, he thought as he studied the door number. It stated fifteen. He remembered that his room was thirteen because he thought of the superstitious nature of it. Rodney was gradually getting less superstitious as he got older. He swung round, the door opened with a slight click. The cold hit him hard. The automatic light came on along with the air conditioning, which he immediately switched off. The window was wide open. A slight breeze was all he felt as he tentatively slammed the window shut. That's funny, he thought. Who the hell left that wide open? Rodney knew his own mind. He was always wary of anything that he did when drunk. He always remembered what he said, although it was not always decipherable. He turned the heater on, then slumped into bed. That's funny. Why do I not feel tired? Normally a few pints would put Rodney out for the count as soon as his head touched the pillow. He puffed up the pillow, sighed deeply and lay down. No sooner had he done this when a loud, irritating noise occurred, like the scratching of long nails on a blackboard. Rodney sat up, alert. He leant over and flicked the light on to reveal a disembodied hand with blood flowing from the fingertip, writing the word "Hell", in blood.

Chapter 2

Sharon had a worried look about her. Where is Rodney? she thought to herself. Normally he would have phoned her by now. She reached for the telephone. Nine-nine-nine was hastily rung.

'Emergency, which service?'

'Police please,' said Sharon. The pause seemed endless as she waited with baited breath. 'Hello, my husband's been gone now for several hours and I am worried sick.'

'Do you know his last whereabouts?'

'Yes, Leamington Spa.' She gave a heavy sigh as the calming man's voice went through the usual procedure.

Meanwhile, Rodney was making his way out of the hotel. He ran into a rotund gentleman and with no apology he entered the lift. Nothing was working. He tried again, but still the lift failed. 'Damn and blast,' he said aloud. He searched for the stairs and saw the sign. He was not too happy as it led him past the room he had just left. He raced as fast as he could to the stairway. He tugged at the door and ran down the stairs, falling on the last three. He pulled himself up on the door handle and rubbed his damaged ankle.

'Good morning, sir,' said a very smartly dressed man.

Totally ignoring the gent, he raced to the rotating door. The fresh air made him all the more drunk. My car, where is my car? he thought. Suddenly, he remembered and ran. As he did so, he questioned why he was now running. So he slowed to a fast walk.

What now? he wondered. Where do I go? My wife is sure to go to the cops. Rodney found his car as his only logical thought that entered his head all night came and went. He eased himself into the car and clasped the keys, which came readily into his hand. He looked round uneasily to see if there were any police around. The car started and leapt into action. Rodney was on a mission to escape from everything that was familiar to him, not liking what life was throwing at him at the moment. Faster and faster the car went for no apparent reason, exiting the town and making for quietness. But it was not meant to be. Just as he felt a little at ease, a police van approached from behind. Without thinking, Rodney pushed his foot hard onto the accelerator. His Peugeot 405 roared smoothly into action. The relatively straight road seemed very bendy as the car screeched from side to side. The police were nearing him gradually. The Peugeot purred all the more as it easily touched 130 mph. Oh no! Rodney thought as he saw the "bends ahead" sign. As soon as he saw the notice, the first bend was upon him.

  He applied his brakes hard deliberately, so that the police van would crash into his rear. The servo assisted brakes did a sterling job. The policeman who was driving did not notice the sign and smashed straight into the back of the car. The headrests saved Rodney's neck. He was unhurt. He put the car into full throttle and left the carnage behind.

  The policeman who was driving was dead instantly. The passenger lifted what was left of his arm tentatively towards the phone, but his hand fell just before he could grasp it. His heart gradually failed and he breathed his last.

  Rodney swerved from side to side as he entered a small village. Smoke was filling the inside of the car, along with the smell of petrol. The car began to splutter and slow unevenly. It was lucky, the car stopped instantaneously, just before an horrendous curve in the road. He struggled to open the slightly damaged door — it screeched open. Then he pushed the car to the grass verge. Rodney grabbed his torch from the glove compartment. Suddenly, from both directions, he saw two police cars with their lights flashing. He darted into the entrance to a churchyard and hid behind some headstones. The cars both stopped at exactly the same time. Then Rodney decided to make for the church door, gambling that it was unlocked. He felt naked to them as he ran awkwardly to the door. It was unlocked and he got inside as the first policeman got out of his car. Rodney walked warily towards the front of the church. It was a dilapidated church. Water dripped slowly through the roof. He tentatively switched on his torch and aimed it towards the ground. The windows to the sides were large stained glass. So he turned it off again. He heard the policemen muttering to one another, then doors slamming. Both cars sped off.

Rodney gave a large sigh of relief He switched the torch back on. It lit up almost the whole church as he raised it upwards. He noticed that at the front end there was a large cabinet, revealing all manner of trinkets, crosses and the like. A large cross was bolted to the floor. A massive selection of coloured photos of famous people who had come to know Christ was to one side of the cross. Rodney looked intently at the photos, and as he did so, the torch beam curved and went onto him as a wonderful smell hit his nostrils. This lasted fifteen seconds, then the scent went away. Rodney got down on his knees, feeling elated and said, 'Thank you Lord Jesus, thank you. Amen.'

Suddenly, Rodney switched off his torch and fell asleep.

It was five o'clock when Sharon received a phone call from the police. She reached eagerly for the receiver. 'Hello,' she quickly said.

'Hello, this is Chief Inspector Mike Sutherland here. Your husband has been involved in an accident, but it appears that he is all right.'

There was a pause. 'Can I speak to him please?'

'I'm afraid we do not know of his whereabouts, madam.'

'Oh,' came the reply.

'Can you tell us what he was wearing?'

'A dark blue coat. Other than that, I-I-I don't know,' she stammered.

'Well, I'm sorry to ring you at this late hour.'

'Oh, that's quite all right, officer,' she blurted.

'Goodbye, madam.'

'Goodbye.' Sharon switched off the light with a worried look on her face.

Rodney awoke. He could see the time on his watch, it was eight o'clock. He could hear police talking inside the church. He maintained his lying position on the pew.

'It doesn't appear that he has been around this area,' one said.

'Yes, he's probably long gone.'

One of the policemen strolled to within inches of Rodney. He stopped, then swivelled on his feet and walked back. Rodney wanted to sigh but dared not to.

'Come on, let's go. These churches give me the creeps.'

The sun shone through the stained glass windows onto him. He sat up wearily. The door to the church was banged hard. Police lights swirled around the inside of the church. Rodney felt he had to make a quick getaway. He noticed a big sign which stated that "Everyone must first plead for forgiveness and then be baptised before they can go to Heaven". This shocked him. He couldn't go anywhere with the police outside. Feeling very dazed with the extreme hangover, he wearily laid down again. The sound of policemen and women disrupted his slumber from time to time.

He awoke three hours later feeling a lot better. The previous day's events hit him hard. What have I done? I've gone from being an innocent man to a raving lunatic all in one day! The sound of the police had gone and there were no flashing lights. He felt relieved. 'I need fresh air,' he decided. Jumping to his feet, Rodney walked to the door, and without hesitation, opened it. Suddenly the sunlight caught his eyes. The glare blinded what was before him. He reached for his sunglasses. He squinted to see his car still on the verge. He decided not to approach it. Rodney turned and ran through the churchyard, between a gate and down a quaint footpath with fields either side. He came to a white bridge and stopped over it. Rodney always felt calm when watching a river. This he needed, his nerves were on edge, he was wandering aimlessly. He looked up and in the distance saw a railway station on the edge of a little village. He strolled towards the village. Noticing a post office, he decided to get a newspaper. The doorbell ringing awakened him fully. He acknowledged an elderly lady as she passed him. 'Good morning,' he said politely to the shopkeeper. He was also old, with prominent crow's feet. He was wearing glasses which were perched on the tip of his nose.

'Good morning, sir. How may I help?'

'Just this,' said Rodney holding up a newspaper. He paid the man, and without saying thanks, he turned to a cash dispenser. He fumbled nervously for his wallet and taking the card he pushed it into the machine quickly. He knew that he only had twenty pounds left, so he was eager to get more out to sustain him. After drawing out £200, he said, 'Thanks, goodbye.'

The man behind the counter said, 'Thank you, cheerio.'

Rodney made for the door. His heart sank as a police car pulled up on the opposite side of the road, but he proceeded to walk out of the door, marching briskly away from the car towards the railway station. He entered the station grounds out of sight of the police car. Not once daring to look round, he swaggered into the booking office as if nothing had happened. A lady with pronounced make-up smiled broadly at him. She was nineteen. He caught the smell of her perfume. She said, 'Can I help?'

Rodney was besotted by her. 'Yes.' Thinking fast, he thought of the furthest place he could. 'Can I have a ticket to Inverness, please?'

'Yes certainly, sir,' she replied. She handed the ticket to him, and grinning from ear to ear, said, 'Have a bonnie wee time, sir.'

He smiled back. Their eyes fixed on each other, he asked, 'What time does the train come?'

'If you keep talking you'll miss it. Five minutes' time, sir.'

'Thanks a lot.' Rodney could not believe his luck. Stepping in wide strides, he made for the ticket collector.

'Platform one,' said a man sternly.

He walked up the stairs and sat on a bench next to a woman in a small fur coat and little else. Rodney eyed her up and down. She ignored him as he gave a heavy sigh. Unfolding the newspaper, he concentrated on the lead story. The train which Rodney required pulled in. He looked at the girl as she stepped into the carriage and followed her to the seat. He sat down beside her and fixed his sight on a sign inside. The train pulled away as a policeman rushed onto the platform.

A rapid thud hit the door of Rodney's house. His wife leapt to her feet and hurried to the door. Opening it, she saw a stocky policeman with a fiercely serious face. Behind him was a shy looking policewoman. 'Please come in,' said Sharon.

'Thank you,' replied the policeman.

Sharon stood still in the lounge. 'Please sit down,' she said, looking at them both for an inkling of what they may say.

'In the accident last night, two of our officers were killed outright and it appears that your husband was responsible.'

Sharon sat down, astonished at the terrible news. 'Why was he responsible?' she demanded.

'The car that he was driving braked suddenly and the police car went straight into the back.'

'But that's not my husband's fault.'

'I'm afraid he was speeding very excessively,' he said sternly.

'Where is he?' she asked.

'He appears to be somewhere near to Bishops Tachbrook. The trouble is we don't know his appearance. Can I have a recent photo of him please?'

'Yes, certainly,' Sharon said in a courteous fashion. She got up eagerly and opened a drawer. 'There you are.' A large photograph was handed to the policeman.

'Thank you, madam. We won't keep you any longer. As soon as we hear of his whereabouts we will be in touch.' He turned and gestured to the policewoman to go on ahead of him.

'Goodbye,' she said sweetly to Sharon.

'Bye,' she replied.

The policeman walked away without a word. He turned and looked solemnly at Sharon. 'Sorry,' said Sharon. She shut the door gingerly, walked into the kitchen and wept, putting her hands to her head.

Rodney awoke. The train had hit a rough bit of track which jolted his head. The police now had his features screened on every computer throughout the land. Railway stations were targeted.

As the train entered Inverness, he noticed three policemen looking intently at his carriage. He rose to his feet slowly. Moving to the door opposite the side where the platform was, he quickly opened the door and jumped down. Suddenly, a train was before him going at a frightening pace. He quickly grabbed onto the wheel of the stationary train. He heaved a sigh of relief, then the train that he was holding on to started to move. He caught his hand. Blood poured from it. Rodney quickly ran to the other side, jumping up the platform as many people looked on, peering backwards to see if the train had left the station. It had. He was exposed to the police. The police ran across the lines. Rodney barged past many people. The police were nearing fast. He ran to the top of the stairs. As the police reached the stairs, he grabbed a big tea dispenser on a trolley and pushed it as hard as he could down the stairs. A policeman got badly scalded. One pulled out his phone and radioed for help. Rodney leapt out of the railway station and grabbed a women from out of her car like a man possessed. He pushed her to the ground and put the car into action. The Metro wheel-spun out of the car park. A policeman stopped and asked the young lady what had happened.

'A man grabbed me from my car.'

'What car is that?' the policeman blurted.

As she explained, Rodney was going out of the town. His car went sideways onto a kerb. He decided to slow to a sensible speed, knowing full well that the police would be on the alert for him. Rodney noticed a sign for the airport. Shall I go abroad? he wondered. Yes, it's my only chance.

Rodney put his foot onto the accelerator more and more as he went through the airport grounds. He slowed the car majestically and got out in the short stay car park. Swaggering along to the main terminal building, he noticed a police car pulling up. Slowly, he altered his direction away, going through a walkway and out towards a small aircraft hangar. He looked shiftily around and saw a small hole in the fence. If only I could get between this small gap first, he mused. His large paunch stopped him in his tracks. He eased his body through the gap, catching his jumper on a jagged bit of wire. His blood-covered hand eased the wire away. His intention was to smuggle himself into a large plane. He crept along the inside of the fence. He looked through a window into a dark room, seeing a large Alsatian dog there. He quickly moved away before the dog turned around to see him. As he edged his way along the shed, he scratched the wood. Suddenly, he heard sniffing. Oh no, the dog! he thought. He rushed out into the view of people wandering around. Suddenly, the dog started to bark loudly. Rodney tried to look inconspicuous by walking in a mild-mannered fashion. The Alsatian's barks went on without any attention from anyone except Rodney. As he waltzed past some people, he noticed a small plane ticking over with no one inside. A man was tinkering with the rear of the craft. Without a moment's hesitation, he was inside the plane. He had no idea what to do. He closed the door just slightly, not wanting to grab the attention of the gentleman behind him. He meddled with various apparatus, but to no avail. Suddenly, the plane leapt forward. The man fell away from the plane. Rodney pushed the plane to maximum revs, going as fast as he could. The man picked himself up and brushed himself down as he ran to the nearby office. As he opened the door, his friend said, 'What's wrong?'

'Someone's stolen my plane,' he said, gasping for breath. 'Look, he's heading straight for the main runway. He'll get himself killed.' He picked up the phone. 'Hello, hello control tower. What do I do? There's an idiot propelling the plane to the main runway.'

'Calm down, sir. What plane?' said the man lackadaisically.

'Oh, forget it,' he said, slamming down the phone. He wiped his brow with his oily hand. 'What do I do? Who do I contact, Bob?'

Rodney reached the beginning of the main runway, almost hitting the wing onto the tarmac as he cornered without hardly slowing. I have got to keep going as I am. I don't know how I have achieved this speed, but no way am I going to stop the momentum. I must get out of this godforsaken country.

The plane went faster and faster. The man who was so calm in the control tower saw the plane that Rodney was piloting and shouted out at the top of his voice, 'Concorde is about to crash into that plane.' Rodney's plane was just about to take off when Concorde came over the top of him to land. He just let go of all the controls, panic-stricken. The plane came to a standstill. Madness, he thought to himself, sheer madness. Why did I risk my life like that? Immediately, a Land Rover pulled up beside him. A man was sitting in the car with his head swaying from side to side. He got out holding his mobile phone to his ear. Why didn't I keep on going? thought Rodney. I could have still taken off after that plane went over the top of me.

The man raced round the plane and opened the door. 'What the bloody hell were you playing at, mate?'

Rodney was in no mood for talking. He kicked the man's face as hard as he could and jumped on his chest, winding him.

Chapter 3

Rodney raced to the Land Rover, jumping in as two other Land Rovers came up fast behind him with lights flashing. He raced the car as fast as he could up the runway, switching off the flashing lights of his vehicle as he headed towards the taxiing Concorde, swerving to avoid it. The Concorde braked to a standstill. The passengers onboard were thrown forward by the impact, the seat belts saving them from harm. The two cars chasing him went either side of the plane.

'I've got him,' said one over-eager driver as he came alongside Rodney. Seeing cars running near to where he was, Rodney pushed the car over some grass. I have got to get out of here and onto that road, he thought determinedly. The car slowed to a snail's pace as the sodden grass impeded Rodney's progress. Both the other cars followed Rodney onto the turf. Damnation, thought Rodney to himself, I am never going to break through this fence going at this speed. Gradually, both following vehicles came to a standstill, one spinning both rear wheels furiously. Rodney noticed the fact that his car had turbo and four-wheel drive, which he was relieved to see. As he looked behind he noticed the sad sight of people kicking their cars and frowning with arms shaking at him. Suddenly, his car raced at a much higher pace. Rodney realised he was on the tarmac again and gaining speed fast. He aimed the car headlong at a fence, knowing that this was his only chance of escape. This is a tough car, I know I can make it, I know I can, he thought. The vehicle pranged into the perimeter fence and gradually screeched through. Scratches covered the paintwork and an obvious large dent adorned the frontage. The car slowly edged onto the kerb side. Rodney gave a large audible sigh of relief. The road was clear. He put the car into full action, going in a direction unknown to him. He was just glad to be away from everything. Almost straight away he saw a sign for a little village and quickly turned the wheel. The car slowed to a snail's pace through the twisty lane. As he hit the village called Warmundsly, he saw the sun shine a radiant glare onto this lovely place. He eased the car over a quaint bridge and looked down at the fuel gauge, which registered empty. He saw a petrol garage right beside him. What a stroke of luck, he declared to himself and swerved the car into place on the forecourt. As he filled the Land Rover, he noticed a large freehouse opposite with the prettiest flowers growing around it. The pub had a "vacancies" sign written largely on a window. Rodney couldn't believe his luck. He was elated. He finished filling the car and paid the man at the counter with a cheery, 'Thanks.'

As he wandered back to his car, his thoughts returned to his wife and child. Will she understand my actions? Will she ever forgive me? Then he thought to himself, what's going to happen to me? He came down to earth with a bump. Rodney locked the car and walked to the public house. As he opened the decidedly squeaky door, a large array of people looked up. Oh no, I want quietness, not this, he thought. He nervously asked the barmaid who looked at him over-attentively, 'Can I have a room for two nights please?'

'Certainly you can,' said the over-friendly girl. 'We have various rooms available.'

'Just a single room please,' he said shyly.

'It's twenty-five pounds,' she replied.

Rodney paid the girl quickly and asked, 'Where can I park my car?'

'Just to the side there is a long lane which goes to the rear of this house. Here are your keys, the room is right in front of you as you get to the top of those stairs,' she stated as she pointed to her right.

'Thanks,' Rodney said.

He received a piece of paper from her. 'All you need to know is on that sheet. What's wrong with your hand?' she enquired, looking at Rodney's hand.

Rodney examined his right hand. Blood was still dripping. 'Oh, I caught it on my car engine,' he lied.

'Here, borrow this.' She handed him a first aid kit from beneath the counter, then turned to another customer who was holding up a fiver impatiently.

Rodney walked away.

After collecting his car from the petrol station, he drove to the car park. Eagerly, he got out of the car and searched around to see that no one was looking. It was a secluded parking point and he tried to remove the stickers from the side of the Land Rover, but with little effect. There were blood marks, which were making matters worse, and he wiped them away with a bandage from the kit. He gave up and jogged to the front of the public house, walking through the lounge and up the stairs. He opened the door to his room and quickly slammed it shut behind him. Whilst in the room, Rodney washed the wound. Oh no, what a mess, he pondered. Should I go to a hospital and get it stitched up? He decided definitely not to, winding cotton wool around the bandage, cutting plasters and securing them to the bandage. He decided to give the kit back straight away. Looking through the window, he saw that the sun was going down. It can't be that late! He opened his cuff button to see his timepiece. 'Four! It can't be four!' he gasped. Well, time for me to get pissed, he thought. He didn't feel tired but was bothered by the day's events.

Pacing down the stairs, he passed a young woman who squeezed past. 'That's unlucky,' she said.

'It wasn't for me,' he said with a glint in his eyes. She blushed and giggled, then went on her way fast. Rodney gaped at her rear.

He perused the people around him. As he neared the bar, a man looked him straight in the eye. Rodney sat down at the bar feeling a tad uneasy. He waited for the barmaid to finish serving others and then passed the first aid kit over to her.

'Is that better?' she said in a concerned manner.

'I'm fine now,' he said with a smile. 'Can I have that stout please?' He pointed to a pump.

'Half or pint?' she said dryly.

'Pint please.'

She handed the pint to him. 'That's two pounds please.'

Rodney gave the lady the two pounds and joked, 'Keep the change.'

She rolled her eyes as if he was round the twist and went on to her next client. Rodney thought to himself, she reckons I'm mad, I wonder if I am? He gulped the drink in haste and pulled out of his pocket the piece of paper that had been given to him by the barmaid. 'Breakfast between seven and nine.' Rodney read. They'll be lucky, he laughed to himself. He took in all that was written on the paper, and as he replaced it in his pocket, a man sat down beside him.

'You're not stopping here are you?' the man asked.

What a cheek! Rodney thought. 'Yes I am,' he replied.

The man was smartly dressed in a suit with black tie and matching shirt. 'It's haunted you know,' he smirked.

'Oh,' said Rodney, not in the slightest bit bothered. 'Can I have another please?' Rodney said to the lady as he supped his last bit of beer.

'I will get that,' said the stranger.

'Oh thanks.' Rodney looked into the man's eyes suspiciously.

'Are you here long?' asked the man.

I'd better be careful now, I don't want to give the game away, Rodney thought. 'Just tonight,' he said quickly.

The man asked the barmaid for a whisky and waited for her to pour it. 'What are you having?' he said to Rodney.

'A Caffreys,' said Rodney, relaxing a bit.

'A .. .' said the man.

The barmaid interrupted. 'I know, a Caffreys.' She poured it out and handed it over.

The stranger handed over a ten pound note and as he received the change, he said to Rodney, 'Let's cut to the chase.'

'Oh thanks,' said Rodney, holding up his pint momentarily.

The girl who had passed Rodney as he was going down the stairs snuggled up to the stranger. He wrapped his arm around her. 'How would you like this girl for the night?'

Rodney didn't know whether or not he was joking. He looked at them both, analysing their faces. Neither were laughing. Rodney sipped his drink.

'One hundred pounds the night.'

Rodney had another sip. The girl smiled with an eager look about her. He pondered for a while. I don't want to offend the girl and then again, I don't want to lose my wife, he thought to himself.

'I'm waiting,' said the man impatiently.

'No sorry, I am married.'

'Sod you then,' said the man, moving away to another point of the bar with his woman. The girl kept looking over to Rodney, smiling all the time. She got her drink and winked at him. Rodney was besotted by her, but his hands were tied. She's gorgeous, he mused. He felt tired. He gave an audible yawn and decided to have an early night. He left the lounge, and as he mounted the stairs, he thought, at least I can no longer be tempted, looking at the man and girl as he went on his way. They both looked at him and laughed loudly.

As he entered his room, he thought of them laughing at him. Whilst getting ready for bed, he kept thinking of them laughing and looking at him. As soon as his head hit the pillow, he was asleep. In his dream he sewed up the hem of the dress in his job as a dress designer and maker. It was tea break. He left the shop area and entered the factory where all of his designs were being manufactured. A new girl had just been employed. He sat opposite her. She was petite. She's cute, he thought. Being manager and owner, he never liked to converse much with staff. He went back to the shop where his assistant was smirking at him. 'You like that new starter, don't you?'

Rodney didn't have a clue how he knew this, but he uttered, 'Yes.'

'Let's make some clothes for her,' his colleague suggested.

'Okay,' agreed Rodney.

Gradually the shop became chock-a-block with various little garments and a few dresses. They were both working like Trojans and the shop became packed with friendly looking people. Rodney looked around to see the new girl squatting on the floor smiling broadly. Customers that seemed familiar to him, kept putting the little items around his neck and then the factory staff gradually came in. People were smothering him from time to time. Rodney looked down and he was almost naked. His shirt was being taken off. He looked at the girl that he fancied again and she was smiling all the more. A blush came to her face. Rodney, feeling embarrassed, walked from shop to shop. All were small, selling various things that were similar to those Rodney sold. He became lost and confused. Everyone was joining in the fun. He eventually found his own shop front and went in. The girl remained sitting on the floor; her blushes were gone Rodney noted.

The coverage of his private parts was becoming scarce. His assistant kept saying, 'You like her don't you?' Rodney was now becoming livid. He was on the ground and he kicked at his two most loyal servants. They both left the shop. As he looked at the array of suspender belts, bras, stockings etc., he became more and more angry. The newcomer still continued to look at Rodney longingly with the sweetest smile that he had ever seen. But he was still mad. People who were mostly all familiar to him kept him on the ground. This infuriated Rodney all the more.

Suddenly, many men came in. One was Rodney's personal assistant and he didn't look too happy. All had a look of hate about them. One came to the side of him and produced a flick knife. 'How would you like to see some blood?'

Rodney was now scared. He clasped his hands together and said aloud, 'Lord Jesus Christ, please save me from these people. Amen.' Immediately he awoke. It was all a bad dream. Prayers do work then, he thought. I am still tempted to go downstairs after that girl though. With that he went to sleep.

A knock on the door awoke Rodney. 'Breakfast,' called a

female voice. He looked at his watch to see that it was half past seven. Feeling alert and calm, he slipped on his clothes and opened the curtains to a sunny day. Stretching his arms wide, he yawned loudly. Rodney opened the door and descended the stairs. As he reached the bottom step, he couldn't believe what he saw. The same man and woman were seated at the same place at the bar, in exactly the same position. The girl said, 'Hiya.'

Rodney replied, 'Hello.'

The man with her said, 'You can still have her you know.'

Rodney did not know what to say and carried on walking. The couple giggled to each other.

'Sit anywhere, sir,' came a voice from behind the counter.

'Oh thanks,' replied Rodney. As soon as he sat down, the girl who had just said hi sat down facing him.

'I hope you don't mind me joining you.'

'No, no not at all.' Rodney was taken aback.

The woman behind the bar said, 'It's a set breakfast, I'll just be one second.'

Rodney glared into the young girl's eyes, then turned to see if her friend was still at the bar. He was nowhere to be seen. 'It's a nice day,' said Rodney tentatively.

'It's a lovely day,' she smiled. 'What's your name?' she asked with a flick of her blonde hair.

'Rod,' he stated quickly.

'Oh, I'm Jude.'

'Not rude Jude I hope.' He laughed and she laughed also. He looked deeply into her eyes.

'Are you staying long?' she asked.

'No, I am leaving in a moment, as soon as I have had my breakfast.'

'Can I come too,' she blurted. Rodney was shocked. 'You

see, I'm a free agent. I just travel around with my case from place to place.'

'Oh I see.'

There was a pause. Rodney was thinking, she is a very attractive girl, but what do I tell her I do? Thinking on his feet he told her that he was on holiday. The woman gave both of them breakfast. 'I hope you enjoy your meal.'

'Thanks,' they both said in unison. Rodney couldn't believe his luck. A lovely girl, nice meal and a delightful day. He started to wonder what the girl was after.

'If you want you can tag along,' he replied to her earlier question.

'Oh thanks,' she said in a blasé fashion, and started eating.

Rodney was ravenous and ate very fast. She must be some sort of hooker, he thought.

She looked to see the ring on Rodney's finger, but said nothing. He must be married, but what the heck. If he's game, so am I she thought.

'Okay, are you ready?' he asked after a while.

'Sure, just gotta get my things,' she stated as she walked up the stairs. 'I won't be long,' she shouted.

What do I tell her and worse still, what do I tell my wife if she finds out that I am giving a girl a lift, Rodney thought. He sipped what was left of some tea and went over to the bar. 'Thank you,' he said to the woman who was cleaning some glasses.

'Oh, that's quite all right. Are you off now?'

'Yes,' Rodney said in a quizzical fashion.

Jude ran down the stairs, went past Rodney and said, 'Come on then.' She giggled. 'Goodbye,' she said to the woman.

'See you,' said Rodney.

'So where are you off to?' asked Jude.

'Oh, I'm just winging it,' he said. 'I just go where the fancy takes me,' he added.

'This your car?' she said.

'Yes,' said Rodney.

'So what do you do?'

'Oh, I deliver these types of vehicles to various places,' he said, lying through his teeth.

They both jumped in and Rodney drove out of the pub car park, heading towards Inverness without realising it.

'I've got to go to a chemist if that's all right,' she stated.

'Yes, I'll drive slowly, there might be one local,' he said.

'No, there's not one in the village,' she insisted.

'Okay,' he replied.

As he drove out onto the main road, Rodney's heart started to pound when he saw a police car going in the opposite direction.

'That's the car we want,' said one of the officers in the police car excitedly. The other policeman swung the car around and gave chase.

Rodney put his accelerator hard to the floor and overtook three cars. 'Hey, what's going on?' said a concerned Jude.

'I've got coppers after me. It's a long story but I'm innocent,' he said in a panicky voice.

What have I let myself in for? thought Jude to herself. 'What are you supposed to have done?' she asked inquisitively.

'I'll tell you later,' he snapped.

'No, tell me now. No wonder you were so quiet at breakfast.'

Rodney became flustered. 'Do you want to get out now?' he blurted.

'No, it's all right,' she said reassuringly. I could do with a bit of action in my life, she mused.

They entered Inverness and Rodney had to slow down to

fifty miles per hour.

One of the policemen following tried to overtake him. The other policeman was on the radio. 'He's going straight for the bridge,' he said to various other vehicles converging on Rodney. But Rodney saw well ahead and slowed slightly to turn the car into a side street. He looked at Jude in a concerned way. A car was swerved past, his foot pressing further on the accelerator. The police car was approaching him fast. Rodney pushed his car all the more. He went straight over a main road, just missing two vehicles going in either direction. The car hit the side of another vehicle as he squeezed in between two. He steered round a corner at breakneck speed, only to find it was a dead end. There was a skip at the end with boards going up. Rodney prodded the accelerator down to maximum speed.

'What, are you going mad?'

But before he could answer, the car hit the boards of the skip and they flew, clipping the top of a wall slightly. The car landed head first on top of a car which was going along a motorway. The vehicle, still going along with the car on top, steadily stopped. The car beneath was crushed and the man driving killed outright. Amazingly, Rodney and Jude were unhurt. They immediately got out of the wrecked Land Rover.

'Now will you tell me what's going on?' asked a shaken Jude.

'Come on,' said Rodney, unaffected by the crash. He grabbed her by the hand and they both dodged the traffic that were sounding their horns. There was a high wall ahead of them, so they raced along the hard shoulder. A slightly broken fence was ahead of them. 'Come on, we can get through here,' he said, pointing to the fence. He grabbed two pieces from the bottom and heaved them up. They both snapped in two halfway up. 'Come on,' he said, going first.

'No, I won't,' she replied, totally bemused by what had happened.

'Come on,' he repeated.

She decided to follow and ripped her skirt on a nail. 'Bloody hell,' she yelled.

'Come on,' he repeated again.

'Is that all you can say?' she said.

They found themselves in a car lot of a Volvo dealership. Most of the cars were ticking over to stop the batteries from going dead. Rodney couldn't believe his luck. He crouched down as he saw a man getting out of a car nearby. Jude followed his example. 'Right, as soon as we can, we're going for that car at the front.'

'Okey dokey,' she said in a facetious manner. This chap's crazy, she thought. Do I go along with this, or do I tell this chap in the car what's going on?

Rodney made for the car, crouching all the way. He looked behind him to see that Jude was still there. He signalled for her to follow. She decided to catch up with him. He pointed to the passenger door and went around to the driver's door. It was open. He climbed inside and waited for her to get in. She gingerly got in. Rodney slowly eased the car off the forecourt as the man who had been starting the vehicles ran towards them from behind, shaking his fist. Rodney sped away in the estate car. As soon as he was a mile away, he slowed to a snail's pace so as to be inconspicuous. Meanwhile, the man back at the Volvo garage alerted the police force that a car had been stolen from his fleet.

'Do you know the vehicle's registration mark?' enquired the policeman at the other end of the phone.

'No, I'll have to check my list. I will get back to you shortly. Who shall I speak to?'

'Can't you stay on the line while you sift through your files?'

barked the agitated policeman.

The car salesman walked speedily towards his showroom. 'Okay, I'm just approaching my computer terminal now.' He sat down on the plush leather seat and rotated it so as to face the computer. 'It's just a question of elimination,' he assured the frustrated policeman.

'Good. We know who he is, but did you get a good look at the woman with him?'

'No, sorry, it all happened so quickly,' the salesman replied in a very apologetic fashion. 'Ah, here we are, we happen to be in luck, there is only one yellow car. Are you ready for this?'

'Yes, fire away,' said the policeman tapping discontentedly on his desk.

'The registration number is ST03 19A and the chassis number is…'

'No, it's all right, that's all we need,' interrupted the policeman as he passed the piece of paper on to over-anxious police officers.

'Goodbye,' said the flustered salesman.

Sharon was just about to finish mopping the floor when the phone rang. She rushed to pick it up in the hope that it was her husband. 'Hello.'

'This is PC Davidson here. I'm just keeping you up to date with what is happening with Rodney.'

'Oh yes,' she said eagerly, expecting good news.

'I am afraid three people in total have been killed by your husband's driving.' There was a pause. 'Hello, are you still there?' Still, there was no sound from Sharon. Her hand was shaking. She sat down, dropped the receiver to the floor and broke down crying. 'Hello, hello?' He turned to his fellow officer. 'We had better get over there, she has gone cold on me.'

Chapter 4

'What is wrong with you? You're crazy,' Jude asked and answered at the same time.

'Are you trying to dampen my ardour?' said Rodney whilst swerving the estate car.

'No, I'm just trying to pick your brain.'

'Leave it, I've got too much on my mind right now.' Rodney wasn't joking either. His thoughts turned from where he was heading to where it was going to end and then to what was to become of his marriage.

Sharon lay crying her eyes out on the kitchen floor. A frail tap on her door was just about audible. Sharon rose gradually to her feet. She was drawn and tired. She opened the door, knowing that it wasn't Rodney as he would have a key.

'Hello, are you all right? We were worried,' said the short, young-looking policeman. He was gaunt looking and balding badly.

'Come on, sit down,' announced an equally short policewoman. She led her to a chair.

'I'm sorry,' said Sharon. 'I should have let you know what was happening. I just became numb I suppose.' There was a long pause. 'Will he go down for this?' She was almost afraid to ask.

'Well, I'm not the best person to ask,' he replied. Scratching his chin, he continued, 'What has happened here is totally out of character, so it is likely that he would have to spend some time in a mental institution. His record shows that he is good.' He stopped for a reply, but there was none forthcoming. He went on. 'You've only got to see how much money he has raised for charity.'

This made matters worse. Sharon held her head in her hands and wept uncontrollably. He looked at his colleague as if to say, what have I done?

Rodney had had enough. He turned the car into a hotel driveway. 'I've got to rest,' he said looking towards Jude. He had a very worried look on his face.

'You look terrified,' Jude said.

'I can't go on running and running all of the bloody time,' he shouted whilst thumping the steering wheel. He braked suddenly on the gravel and the car skidded to a halt.

'Please calm down,' Jude pleaded. She was frightened. Her hand touched gently on Rodney's leg.

'I'm sorry, it's just becoming too much.'

'What is?' Jude asked.

'Oh, I don't want to talk about it right now,' he replied.

They opened the doors in unison. Rodney activated the central locking mechanism and the two of them walked wearily towards the hotel. Rodney was happy that the car was out of sight of the main road. Jude and Rodney proceeded into the lobby of the establishment. 'I'll do the talking,' he whispered. She nodded in agreement.

A man with blond hair enquired, 'May I be of assistance?' in a very officious manner.

'Yes, can I have a double room, please.'

'Yes, I think we can run to that. Just the one night is it, sir?'

'Yes,' said Rodney

'There are many variants to your stay, all listed here,' the ageing man said as he handed the booklet to Rodney, his hand shaking nervously. 'Does sir wish to pay by cheque or by cash?'

Quickly Rodney answered, 'Cash,' as he fumbled for his wallet, perspiration telling on his brow. The old man looked at him quizzically. Jude looked a little uneasy, her expression changing from one extreme to another. Rodney produced the wallet and placed it on the counter.

'Oh,' said the man. 'I forgot, you need to know how much.' He tapped away at a rapid pace on the laptop computer. 'That's £109.'

'What?' blurted Rodney. 'That's London hotel prices.'

'Oh sorry, I should have told you, that includes three three-course meals in one day and full use of our fitness club. It's all in there,' he said, pointing to the booklet.

'Oh, I suppose it's good value for money,' he mumbled whilst sighing. He pulled out the exact money and handed it to the gentleman who handed the security card over to Rodney. They carried on with other necessities and when all was done, they walked to their room with the porter. This dude's more aged than him behind the counter, thought Rodney. The baggy-eyed porter limped towards the lift. When they all reached the door, Rodney swiped the card and said, 'That will be all,' to the man, not wanting to give a tip.

'Okay, sir,' he said and wandered off.

Rodney tapped the remote control for the television. 'That alien's an evil demon!' shouted the distraught woman on the TV. Rodney quickly switched channels, he didn't want anything disturbing on.

'Getting to know you, getting to know all about you,' came

a song from a young man.

'Ah, that's better,' said Rodney whilst taking his shirt off. He decided to switch the advert channel on. Rodney loved adverts and particularly this channel as it did only show the most entertaining ones.

Jude put her hand gently on Rodney's shoulder and caressed him. 'Would you like some tea or coffee? She said smoothly.

'No thanks,' he replied.

They were both taking each other's clothes off and soon they were almost naked. Rodney was becoming aroused fast. 'You're gonna burn in hell,' said a man with a growl on the advert channel as an angel ran away. Rodney instantly became upset by this. He started to get dressed again rapidly. 'Sod this, sod this,' he barked. 'I'm outa here.'

'What?' she replied in a surprised manner.

'I'm going,' he said firmly.

'You're not going to leave me?'

'Too right I am. I shouldn't be here with you, I'm a married man.'

'Please don't just leave me here, please don't. You can't, you can't just leave,' she pleaded. She got on her knees.

'Okay, okay, you can come along.'

'Why now? What's wrong?'

'I just saw something on the television that disturbed me.'

'You must rest. It's rest that you need, nothing more, nothing less. You've been on the go all of the time.'

'Okay, all right I'll rest, but no hanky-panky though,' Rodney insisted.

'You've got it,' she said in a thankful way.

They both jumped into bed and Rodney switched the television off.

Rodney awoke with the sound of the telephone ringing. He reached for the receiver. 'Hello.'

'Good morning, sir, this is your breakfast courtesy call.'

'Oh, thank you,' replied Rodney. 'Goodbye,' he said politely. He put the phone down. He had had a good night's sleep and felt a lot better than the previous night. Jude had also awoken and was stretching. As she did so, she patted Rodney's head. 'Oh hello,' he said. 'Shall we go for breakfast?'

'Yes, why not,' said Jude.

Rodney put on the TV and tuned it to a music station. *Could You Be Loved* by Bob Marley was playing. Jude swirled her long, blonde hair and smiled broadly at Rodney. Then she asked, 'Shall I be mother?' as she put the kettle on.

'Yes, why not,' he replied with a grin.

They both got dressed. Rodney looked at the guide book to the hotel as Jude finished preparing the drinks. 'Do you fancy coffee or tea?' she enquired.

'Oh, tea please.' There was a pause. 'What are we going to do now?' he frowned.

Thirty minutes passed and they were sitting in the dining room, still deliberating what to do next. The room was empty apart from an elderly couple. Every now and again they would glance across, but generally speaking they minded their own business. Jude spoke quietly saying, 'Look, I don't want to know your business, all I want is to be with you. I know it sounds like a record.' She smiled and then laughed out loud.

'That's fine with me,' Rodney said. 'I'm not stopping here any longer. I can't afford to,' he asserted as he played with his bacon and egg. Jude sipped the last bit of tea left in her cup. 'Shall we set off now?' Rodney asked.

'Yes,' replied Jude.

'Let's get our things and check out,' Rodney insisted. He just wanted to get back on the road.

'Okay, let's,' said Jude.

Rodney expected something else to come from Jude's lips, but nothing was forthcoming. He got up and pulled back Jude's chair in a gentlemanly fashion. However, all he was interested in was speed. They both walked over to the lift. The lift opened and two young men walked out, laughing merrily. Rodney noted that they were both tall and dark haired. One smiled at Jude. Rodney noticed and felt a little jealous. They stepped in and Rodney pressed their floor button. When they reached their floor, Jude started whistling 'Greensleeves'. They went into the room, gathered up their few belongings and left for the reception. A maid was just about to go into the room as they left. 'Is it all right if I go in?' she asked.

'Sure,' replied Rodney. They both smiled at each other. Jude saw how happy Rodney looked and thought that things would start to quieten down now. How wrong she was.

They walked to the lift and Rodney, as usual, pressed the lift button. It opened immediately. As the door shut and they began descending, Jude noticed a strange expression on Rodney's face. 'Are you all right?' she asked.

'Fine,' came his reply. It was the calm before the storm.

They quickly went to the desk. All staff were busy. Rodney tapped his fingers on the table, his patience was wearing thin. A woman was on the phone, while a man was talking to a customer. Rodney banged the pass onto the counter, rang a bell and shouted loudly, 'Goodbye.'

Jude and Rodney looked at each other, Rodney with a frown and Jude with eyes wide open and raised eyebrows. Everybody in the reception area stopped and looked in Rodney's direction.

'Come on, let's go,' he said, wishing he hadn't done that.

They stepped out into the sunshine, Jude feeling a bit cheated as they hadn't used the hotel to its fullest potential. Rodney pressed the remote locking and they both got into the vehicle. They set off at a nice steady pace.

'Where are we going now?' enquired Jude.

'Down south as far as we can go. Probably Torquay. The police are on to us big style and we need to avoid them at all costs. I'm going to change this vehicle again soon, by fair means or foul.'

'That would get the police even more involved,' replied Jude.

'Don't you think I know that?' retorted Rodney, his voice raised even higher than in the hotel.

'Look, let me out, you've changed,' she insisted.

'No,' said Rodney. 'I know that my cheese has slid off my cracker, but you can get me through this. You're stopping,' he asserted, his hand on the button above the door to stop her side from opening.

'You're stopping you mean,' she said as she pushed the gear lever forward to the sound of metal on metal, grinding badly.

The car juddered to a slow pace and was filled with the smell of smoke and metal. Rodney punched Jude several times. Her face was bleeding from the mouth and the forehead. She slumped unconscious on the door window. The sound of irate drivers shouting abuse at Rodney filled the air and the occasional sound of a car horn blasting made him all the more angry. One man nodding his head made Rodney wind down the window and shout, 'Loser!' He smiled as he said it, a sort of crazy smile that was neither one nor the other. Rodney was now really mad. He went colliding into the car, keeping the same expression — a sickening smile, once to the left wing, then into the rear, then between the doors on the left.

At this, Jude came round. Dazed, she just witnessed Rodney crashing one car, then another, then another. 'Stop, please stop. Why are you doing this?' But no reply was heard. 'No!' screamed Jude as the car hit a Porsche and then a BMW. Blood was now streaming down into her eyes. She knew she had to get out and fast. She pulled up the lock and pushed the door open. Jude had forgotten the seat belt though and Rodney sped up to shut the door.

'Do that again and you'll regret it, I promise you that,' he asserted. Rodney had crashed into another car by then, this time a Mercedes. Then Jude realised — he was just crashing into salubrious cars — not vans, trucks or old cars — just posh ones. She had lost count of how many had been hit, but it was in the twenties.

The road narrowed into a dual carriageway. A man with a mobile phone had got in touch with the police. All of this had happened in just three minutes. The man got through. 'Hello, which service do you require?'

'The police,' the man said. He was shaken up from the collision with his car.

'Okay, putting you through now,' said the operator. 'Hello, police service,' said a very officious man.

'There's a lunatic crashing into vehicles on the southbound M74.'

'It's a big road, sir. Near to which junction?'

'Past junction 14. He's mad, he'll kill someone,' said the man. He was hyperventilating.

'Thank you, sir. Is anybody injured?'

The man looked at his wife. She was holding her arm. Then

he looked at his two children in the back, they were unharmed. He gave a sigh of relief, then said to the policeman, 'We're Okay, but other people seem harmed.'

Behind Rodney's car was utter carnage. 'You're hitting posh cars, you're hitting posh cars,' Jude kept repeating. 'You're hitting posh cars, why are you hitting posh cars?' There was no reply as Rodney carried on hitting cars. Enough is enough, she thought. Within seconds she had the seat belt undone and the door opened, but Rodney was too quick for her and he kept his promise by slamming the car into another vehicle on Jude's side. He trapped her leg and blood came streaming out. She squealed with pain as Rodney grabbed her and pulled her back into the seat. He pulled away fast again to try to bring the door back to closed, but it was barely hanging onto the hinges and was falling off, totally misshapen.

'I warned you,' he snarled. Jude was totally lost for words. She was writhing in pain with blood still pouring out. She ripped her skirt and made a bandage. She knew that sympathy from Rodney would not be forthcoming.

Still the crashing went on, then suddenly a car went into Rodney's, taking him utterly by surprise. A man was trying to bring him to a halt by pushing him into the barriers. Jude was oblivious, she was still trying to put the bandage on. This action brought Rodney to his senses. Now other road users were joining in. A car sped through some of the carnage and came to a halt in front of Rodney and Jude. Rodney smashed into the back of him. Jude went into the windscreen, smashing her nose beyond recognition. Gushing blood. The man got out of his vehicle, waltzed over to Rodney, opened the door and grabbed Rodney tightly by the throat. 'Go up my arse would you?' he said in a Scottish drawl. He kept squeezing and a few people gathered around and started clapping. Some people were angry, others dazed.

'He's mad, he's crazy,' screamed Jude.

'I don't know what came over me,' said Rodney, now shaking with fear. Rodney could see that the Scotsman was of large stature even from close proximity. The clapping continued from some quarters as the Scotsman, loving the attention he was getting, began to shake Rodney by the collar.

Jude said, 'Oh my God, oh my God!' as she surveyed the carnage behind her. Two women came over to comfort her. She looked at Rodney and screamed at him as loudly as she could, 'You'll go down for this.'

A man said, 'Hey, nutter,' and punched him. Then others followed suit.

A cockney man said, 'You bladdy idiot.' Some were lost for words and looked at one another.

A police car pulled up with sirens blaring. 'Your missus is right, you're going down, sonny Jim,' insisted the Scotsman as he pushed Rodney face down on the ground. Sweat came from Rodney's brow.

'All right, we'll take over now, sir, if you don't mind,' said an officer. Two officers grabbed him, one by the legs and one by the arms. By now everyone was in stunned silence as the policeman read him his rights.

A man fumbled for his mobile phone. When it was in his hand, he telephoned for ambulances. Whilst looking at people injured he angrily said, 'Just send as many ambulances as you can. You've not seen anything like this before.'

'Please, help me find my daddy,' said a little five-year-old boy.

As Rodney was being dragged away, a woman came up to

Jude and said, 'I'm a nurse, please let me through.' She walked sideways through the crowd that had gathered.

'You're gonna pay for this, pal,' barked a man to Rodney.

Some men were trying to right an estate car that had been upturned. It came down with a crash. Two women jumped at the sound. It seemed louder than it was as everyone was quiet. 'I'm sorry,' was heard from Rodney's lips. The police car door shut. A cheer or two and the odd sound of clapping came as the police handcuffed Rodney. The sound of distant sirens was heard and then the police car's siren disturbed the troubled crowd. 'Can't you switch that noise off?' shouted Rodney.

The officer got on the phone to say, 'We have apprehended the man and are returning to the station. Stop shouting, you're in enough trouble as it is.'

The police car raced to the police station at breakneck speed. Rodney's contorted face was worrying the driver somewhat. The car screeched around the country lane, the policemen not knowing what would happen next. They were feeling uneasy about the fact that there were only two of them against a madman. Unfortunately for them, Rodney was thinking the very same thing. His mind working overtime, he was thinking that he could escape with just a policeman with him. Rodney forced the handcuffs over the handbrake and pulled hard. He knew that the pain he was feeling would be equal to the pain that the officer was feeling. 'Stop the car!' he demanded.

'No, keep going, Jim,' said the policeman. The driver accelerated all the more. The car was shaking madly, going over the grass verge on many occasions. A tree was just missed.

Rodney pulled all the more. 'Give me the keys,' he insisted.

The policeman was in more agony than Rodney. 'Okay, okay,' he said and handed the key to Rodney who quickly opened the handcuffs. Within seconds the handcuffs were clamped onto the ceiling handle.

'Don't stop!' said the trapped policeman, punching at Rodney.

Rodney was giving as good as he got as he was opening the door, but the car was going too fast and the door shut again.

'We're approaching the station, need urgent assistance,' said the driver in pigeon English.

The two men were fighting when Rodney had the idea of involving the driver in the fray. He managed to get one punch in to the driver's head, but that was all. The officer in the back protected the driver valiantly. 'We need urgent assistance, over,' said the shocked driver going over red lights in the now busy town.

They were now approaching the police station and the car had to slow down somewhat. The policeman in the rear pulled the handle off the ceiling with the handcuffs. Rodney realised this and quickly opened the door, but the policeman put the handcuffs over Rodney's neck, as the police car banged the car door shut against the station's wall, stopping Rodney's escape. The outside of the station was buzzing with police activity. 'The key,' said the officer viciously. Rodney obliged, realising now that the game was up. By now, police were grabbing his arms, even though he was not struggling.

Soon he was in the small two-way mirrored room, deep within the station building.

'You're in big, big trouble now, sunshine,' said an officer.

A commandant walked in, took one look at Rodney and said, 'We need a psychologist.' And turning to a policeman, said, 'Get him.' The commandant looked deep into Rodney's eyes. 'Strap him down — now!' Rodney's mad eyes were not impressing the superior officer. Two policemen went out of the room to get the strapping. 'I want this recording. You get the camera,' he said pointing. He was in no mood for niceties. 'What is it with you? I've just had a computer printout of the damage report on this incident and it makes for gruesome reading. Three people killed and twenty-four injured, most of them badly.' There was silence from Rodney. 'Not speaking, eh?'

Just then two policemen walked in with straps. They quickly tied him up. The commandant said, 'You make me sick.'

'Can I have a cigarette?' said Rodney.

'No you can't,' said the commandant adamantly. His full name was Douglas Gerald Grub. 'As tight as you can,' he asserted whilst pointing to the straps. He was stocky and as hard as iron. Douglas wore a pin-striped suit. His face was red from high blood pressure. His eyes seemed to burn into anyone who dared look into them. He had a pronounced chin.

Just then, the psychologist walked in, a mild-mannered gent called Michael. He took a good look at Rodney, said good morning and looked around at the people in the office. The commandant and the psychologist sat down in unison. Douglas spoke first. 'I don't know what I'm going to charge him with and that's for sure. He just collided with cars.' He looked menacingly into Rodney's eyes. 'Injuring and killing people. You make me sick.'

'Why did you do it?' said Michael, not one to mince his words.

'I don't know, I just lost control I suppose.'

'You suppose?' said the commandant inquisitively.

'Sorry, but let me just have a one to one with this man,' said Michael.

'I wouldn't call him a man for a start,' said Douglas

sarcastically. Michael looked at Douglas with smouldering eyes. 'Okay, okay, you do the questioning,' said Douglas.

Michael glanced at Rodney's hands. They were trembling. 'I can't believe what I've done,' he said. He paused, then spoke again. 'I demand a lawyer.'

Douglas looked over to an officer in the room, pointed to the doorway and said, 'Do the necessary will you, Pete.'

Peter said, 'Sure,' and waltzed out.

'How many cars did you hit?' enquired Michael.

'About twelve I guess,' replied Rodney regretfully.

'Why did you hit them?'

'I know it sounds crazy, but I... I... I was jealous of them having posh cars.

'You were envious? Why were you envious?'

'They had something that I can only dream of I suppose.'

'Oh, he supposes again,' said the facetious commandant.

'Look, I'm not saying another word without a solicitor,' shouted Rodney at the top of his voice.

Michael shot a look of disappointment towards Douglas. 'Get some drinks in, I think we're here for the duration,' Michael said with a serious expression to an officer.

'What about him?' said the officer quickly, looking at Rodney and then glancing into Douglas's menacing eyes.

'What about him?' repeated the commandant as if to say that Rodney was a piece of excrement.

The officer walked out of the doorway, getting the commandant's message loud and clear. Another officer walked into the amply sized room.

'What started all this off?' said Michael, ignoring Rodney's pleas. The psychologist couldn't help himself. He loved his job.

'I was in a book shop. I dropped the Bible on the floor, it

opened to a page that said, "Satan fell to earth like lightning". And the shop just caught fire.'

'Where was this?' asked the eager psychologist.

'Leamington Spa.'

There was silence all round. 'I saw that on the television news,' said Michael. Rodney gave a very visible sigh of relief, as if his problems were now solved. How wrong he was. This was just the start to Rodney's troubles. Michael turned to Douglas and said, 'What we are dealing with here is extreme psychosis caused by a psychosomatic incident. This man is very ill and no solicitor can save him from his fate.'

'You've deduced that from just a few words from him?' asked Douglas.

'Yes,' replied the psychologist.

Rodney's face turned white and from then on he turned into a physical wreck.

'I've just got to have a word with two of my colleagues, then we'll get him into hospital,' said Michael. Rodney slouched and was visibly shaking, his mouth open. 'You'll be all right,' said Michael, not knowing why he said it.

Peter returned with the drinks. 'Cancel the lawyer, please,' said the commandant glaring at the police officer. 'And shut that bloody door, it's like Piccadilly Circus in here.'

'Come with me,' said Michael in an officious manner. 'You and you.' Michael pointed to two officers. 'Come with me, guard him,' he insisted. They walked out into the corridor and Rodney struggled, knowing his fate. They made for Michael's office. Michael stopped and drove his card through the door's lock, then opened the door. They pushed Rodney into the room. 'Please take a seat,' said Michael politely. Rodney obliged immediately. Michael smiled at everyone. He loved the power that he had in his job. He keyed in the number that he wanted, it was the telephone number to Rampton Hospital. 'Hello, this is Michael. Are there any spaces there? I've got a man here who needs urgent attention.'

'Yes, send him right along, we're ready for him,' came the bubbly reply, as if it was good news.

'Thanks, goodbye.'

It seemed so simple. A quick phone call and Rodney was going to be in a mental hospital for a very long time. Rodney waited patiently because Michael just sat there analysing his expressions. Rodney knew that he had done wrong. His face became contorted because he didn't know whether to be happy or sad. This made interesting analysis for Michael and would go into his records. 'Give this man an escort to Rampton with immediate effect,' said the psychologist with a frown. He was analysing Rodney constantly and thinking back to what Rodney had done. Michael hadn't heard the full story, but what he had heard was horrific enough.

Rodney struggled as the two police officers led him out of the office. They walked through just one swing door and the car was waiting for them. The one that was to drive was a stocky man with an expressionless face. He had thick set eyebrows that met in the middle. His moustache was thin and unkempt. He opened the door. Both officers knew nothing of Rodney's history, but they were taking no chances. They both chucked him into the car without ceremony. The policeman who got in the back was blond. He had mad eyes and an attitude to match. His eyes were also widely set apart. He was thin, but had broad shoulders. His strength was phenomenal. Rodney decided that enough was enough. He suddenly became placid. He had suddenly hit a brick wall when Michael dropped the bombshell. He also clocked the police officer in the back seat and the sheer force of him placing the handcuffs on him.

The journey would take an hour and in that short while only a few words were spoken and that was between the two officers. The whole trip was not in the least eventful.

The car stopped for a few seconds at the guard hut. The guard let them through. They stopped with a screech, the driver not taking any notice of the twenty miles an hour speed limit. The hospital staff watched from the doorway as the two policemen escorted Rodney out of the vehicle. They showed little compassion for him as they pushed him into the arms of the staff.

'Now don't struggle,' said an unkempt man with long blond hair that looked more like straw.

'I won't,' Rodney assured him.

The man on Rodney's other side was broad. He looked fat in the face, but had large muscles. Rodney obliged when the large nurse said, 'Walk slowly and do not struggle.' They strolled through an automatic door. It made a hissing sound which disturbed Rodney. His first impression of the hospital was that it was dirty. He looked at a nurse and thought that she was a patient. She was a gaunt woman with a series of moles that had hair coming out from them. A patient glared at Rodney for a few seconds which seemed like minutes to Rodney.

'In you go,' said the blond nurse, whose name was Peter.

They forced Rodney into a room with a nurse who had thick rimmed glasses and an obvious wig. 'Hello, please sit down,' said the man courteously. He gave the impression that he had been expecting him for a long time.

Peter said to the man, 'This is Rodney. He has been killing policemen and other people too.'

'Would you like a drink?' said the nurse to Rodney.

'I'm fine,' said Rodney with a slight stammer.

'Why did you do all this killing?' said the nurse. There was no reply from Rodney, who was too tired to even bother to answer. He had had enough for one day. It showed. The bags under his eyes were large. 'Okay, how did all this start?' Still there was no reply. The two nurses who were guarding Rodney looked at each other as if to say, we've seen all this before. The nurse asking the questions blew air out, his lips protruding. He rolled his eyes around the room and then looked at the two guards. 'Look, this is getting us nowhere. I'll see you in the morning. You're looking tired,' he confirmed. 'Has he got any belongings?' he enquired of Peter.

'No,' came the blunt reply.

'Okay, take him to his dorm. This man needs sleep.'

The two nurses were about to help Rodney up, but he was too quick for them. They both grabbed his arms and Terry, the other nurse, opened the door. They approached the dormitory and Peter pointed to the toilets. 'There's the loos if you need them.' The sun beamed onto the three men from the window.

'This is your dorm,' pronounced Terry.

It was only eleven o'clock in the morning, but Rodney hadn't slept properly for two days and it showed. As soon as his head hit the pillow, he was fast asleep.

It was one a.m. and the nurse woke Rodney to say that he needed a sleeping pill. Rather bemused, he accepted her demands. She handed him a glass of water.

'Haven't you got something a little stronger? Whisky perhaps?' he quipped. She's stunning, he thought.

'Haven't you got a change of clothes?' she asked, pulling her long blonde hair over her head.

Her eyes met Rodney's and there was a gaze between them

that he had never experienced before. They were locked in eye contact for several seconds. It was love at first sight.

'No,' he replied. 'I've only just come in tonight.'

'Oh,' she said in a soft spoken voice. She smiled and her eyes danced. 'What no pyjamas?' she laughed, then proceeded to pull the bed clothes back to reveal Rodney's naked body. Her eyebrows raised and her eyes widened.

'Do you mind?' said Rodney in a posh accent. Surprised by her actions, he slapped her bum as she walked quickly away, flushed red and beaming. He pondered that this couldn't be such a bad gaff and that he had not even asked her name. Lying back on the pillow, he sighed and immediately fell asleep.

He was woken abruptly by a murderous sound from behind the curtains of the dorm. It sounded like someone vomiting and the clatter of tins. He felt disturbed and pulled the pillow over his head. Why can't there be separate rooms? He wondered. Staying in this position for quite a while, he then decided to get up and see if he would see the same nurse again. Sure enough, she was there adjusting a television in a room a little further up the corridor. Dressed in brown trousers and a white top, she looked shapely.

'Hello, my name's Rodney by the way. What's yours?'

'Paula,' she said rising from her askew position.

Rodney became aroused and she noticed. There was no one else in the room, but he still felt a little awkward and covered his indignity.

She smiled broadly and said, 'You haven't had your breakfast yet! It's over there.'

'Oh, keeping your eye on me are you?'

'Yes, of course,' she insisted as if it was obvious.

Paula walked away, but Rodney stayed watching the TV

while his erection diminished. Then, walking over to the dining room, he noticed a man standing against a wall face on. Another was sitting dressed drably and shaking uncontrollably. A male nurse approached Rodney. In a concerned manner he said, 'Cornflakes or a fried meal, sir?'

Rodney presumed that he looked awful. He certainly felt it and was glad to say yes to a fried meal. The nurse obliged by turning and retrieving a large prison-like tray festooned with all manner of goodies. Rodney soon consumed the contents and looking round, noticing the staff checking on him from afar.

Rodney was directed into a gigantic room by a woman who had all of the right things in the right places. She was beauty personified. He looked into her eyes. She shied away, turning her face rapidly. The young girl left the room and Rodney's heart sank.

Soon after, a man walked into the room with Rodney's wife. 'Here is someone to see you,' he said.

Gingerly, Sharon walked into the sparsely furnished room. 'Where have you been, Rodney?' Sharon said exceedingly affectionately.

'I've been on the run.'

'I know, but what from?' There was a deathly silence.

'Questions, questions,' shouted Rodney manically. 'So many questions.'

'I've bought you some nice things,' Sharon said calmingly. She slowly brought a box of chocolates out of a bag. 'I have got these. I thought you would like this.' She revealed a mini disc player. 'And this is your favourite group isn't it?'

'Yes.' Rodney beamed, got up and kissed Sharon on the lips. Then he sat back down again. Sharon sat down next to him. Rodney was now relaxed. He looked up at a dodgy bloke who was peering through the window. 'Piss off,' Rodney said to the man.

'Rodney!' Sharon said, surprised at her husband's outburst. She had been married to Rodney for twenty years and was embarrassed and bemused by his bad language and strange anger that she had never experienced before.

'Oh, and I got you this.' Rodney didn't notice at first. He was too busy looking for the now gone man. Sharon held the photo of them both in front of him impatiently.

Rodney looked at the photo. He stared at it. Excrement came out of his rear orifice. 'I'm going to hell,' he said in a petrified tone.

'Don't talk stupid,' said Sharon, extra concerned for her husband's sanity. She moved closer, cuddling him, not noticing his accident. 'Don't talk so silly.'

'The photo — I've got red eyes.' He pointed, as if she was stupid.

'I know that. They've got special cameras to stop that now.'

'Look, you dotty cow, how come you haven't got red eyes? You're looking directly at the camera lens too. You're going to heaven, but I'm doomed, I'm damned, I'm going to hell!'

All at once, three nurses appeared from three separate directions and grabbed hold of Rodney.

'What is wrong with you?' demanded Sharon. She frowned. A nurse named Agatha shook her head in dismay.

'What happened?' enquired another nurse peering deep into Rodney's eyes.

'He says that he is going to hell because he has red eyes in this photo,' Sharon said to all of them matter-of-factly.

'Oh my God, my God.' Rodney started trembling in a big way. A nurse quickly ran to the phone to ask for help. Agatha and the other nurse grabbed Rodney's arms, which only made matters worse. 'No! No! No!' said Rodney. 'Why me? Why me? Why me?' He slumped to the floor.

'We'll have to accuphase him,' insisted Agatha. 'Yes, here are the men now.'

As soon as this was said, Rodney jumped up and escaped to another dorm as the men chased after him. He looked around and all he could see was a man with an injection squirting into the air, a mean look on a massive man and four others chasing behind him. Rodney pushed over a drinks trolley and scalded himself. He was unaware of his injuries as he paced faster and faster. A nurse in front of Rodney pounced on him and grappled him to the ground. The scene was surrounded by people. Four nurses held him down. 'HELP!' shouted Rodney.

A patient shouted, 'Leave him alone, he's done nothing wrong.'

Rodney was dragged unceremoniously back to his dorm, which to Rodney seemed like an eternity. Finally, he was placed onto his bed. His trousers were yanked from him.

'Ooh, you haven't got any pants on have you, Rodney?' says a nurse.

'No,' said Rodney.

'Now this won't hurt. We are just going to insert a needle into you Rodney.'

'Okay,' said the now placid man.

The next day Sharon entered the hospital. "Rampton Hospital Welcome" said the sign. Sharon thought to herself that it was anything but welcoming. Her car came to a halt in a space that said it was reserved for Doctor Jackson, but she was past caring. She entered the building when her phone rang. 'Hello,' she said.

'It's only me,' said her mother as if it was obvious who it was.

'Oh, hello, Mum.'

'Where are you?'

'Oh, I'm visiting Rodney.'

'You be careful, he's dangerous. I've just been reading about him in the national newspapers.'

'Oh, I didn't realise it was so newsworthy,' said Sharon in a faint voice.

'What are you g... g to d...?'

'You're breaking up, Mum, and I'm not allowed to have a mobile phone on in this hospital any way.'

'Oh all right, I'll see you tonight then.'

'Okay, Mum, bye.' Sharon slammed the phone into her purse. She wasn't in the mood for conversations.

As she entered the lift, a man came out shouting, 'DOG DOG DOG.' Sharon was quick to shut him out. A woman on the floor had an imaginary friend that she was speaking to.

'Have something to eat,' she said. 'Don't be shy.'

Sharon was almost glad to escape into the male dormitory that housed Rodney. I'm afraid that you won't get much out of him,' said a nurse to Sharon. 'He has been accuphased. He'll be out for three days now.'

'Oh, thanks for not telling me sooner. Another wasted journey.' She swivelled around, and without looking at Rodney, walked out.

Three days later Rodney roused himself to the sight of a nurse looking deep into his eyes. 'Hello, good morning,' came the sweet voiced greeting.

'Uh, hello,' came the reply in a gruff tone.

Rodney soon felt refreshed and bright-eyed when the nurse said to him, 'I'll get you a cup of tea,' and off she trundled.

Rodney felt a little embarrassed as he jumped out of bed, because he realised that he was naked. I wonder who undressed me? he thought. Then he vaguely remembered the previous three nights' happenings. 'Oh, you haven't got any pants on,' he recalled. He soon got some clothes on and rapidly made his way towards the nurse by the teapot.

'What time is it?' Rodney enquired.

'It's ten o'clock in the morning, Rodney,' she said nicely.

'Can I have some breakfast please? I'm starving.'

'Yes, of course,' she acknowledged. She handed him the cup of tea, which was in a flowered teacup that Rodney felt was not in keeping with the masculine image which he wanted to portray. The nurse held her arm outstretched and pointed in the direction of the eating area.

Feeling totally alert now, he was soon at one of the dining tables and waited for her to serve him eggs, bacon, fried bread and sausage with tomatoes. Rodney drooled down his chin and quickly wiped it away. The nurse turned with a smile and gave him his breakfast. 'There you are, sir,' she said with a positive glint in her eyes.

'What's your name?' he enquired.

'Susan,' she replied and then walked away.

He pondered how he could escape from this high security hospital all through the meal. Rodney was a born worrier and knew that his time in here was going to be tough and also long. Going away from the table, he surveyed the area. It was built hexagonal so that nurses could deliberately look from one ward to the other. Nobody seemed to look at him apart from the nurses, who analysed his every move. He felt invaded and also did not feel like talking to anyone.

So he felt annoyed when a male nurse said, 'We will be having a meeting with the head psychiatrist in a little while.' He grinned whilst Rodney remained straight-faced. Abruptly, Rodney turned away and wandered around the small area to check out exits and to see where the television was as he thought that he might be featured on the local news. Nobody was in the TV room and Rodney soon became acquainted with the remote control unit. It was the latest in new technology. He knew exactly what to do to gain access to himself on screen. He pressed all of the right numbers etc. and soon, there he was on the screen. He pressed the enter button and saw himself being eased out of the car with a sheet over his head and taken into the police station. As he was watching the carnage that he had caused on the motorway, the presenter said that seven people had died and forty-four were injured. The nurse who had awakened Rodney watched with great interest. Rodney was unaware of her presence. The Scotsman who had manhandled Rodney was talking a lot about how he had grappled Rodney to the ground. Soon there were a lot of people watching the television and as soon as Rodney became aware of this, he hurriedly switched it off. The staff in the room soon knew that Rodney was not to be trusted. They dared not try to regain the station for fear of his actions. Everyone looked at everyone else and there was silence as they all walked away, except Rodney. He held his head in his hands, wondering how he could have made all that happen.

'Doctor Wright will see you now,' said a rather stern, neatly turned out young man with a moustache.

He looks serious, thought Rodney as he got up from his seat. The nurse tried to make conversation with him, but to no avail. He asked if Rodney had had time to wash, but Rodney gave no reply and slightly later he wondered if he had made a mistake by not answering.

Soon they were outside the doctor's room. Two nurses were behind them. One knocked on the door, and without waiting for a reply, they went in.

'Please take a seat,' said the psychiatrist. 'How are you feeling?'

'Well, my nerves send a series of impulses up to my brain,' came the reply.

'Are you being facetious?' said the woman doctor knowingly.

'Yes,' he said and then wondered why he should be so obnoxious. 'Sorry — I am feeling calm.'

'Okay, okay,' said the psychiatrist. 'Why did you do what you did?'

'I don't know, it is completely out of character.'

'And you still feel calm?' she enquired.

'Yes.' There was a long pause and then Rodney blurted out, 'I'm feeling utterly compos mentis.'

'Oh,' came the doctor's reply. 'We're going to keep you in for a long time you know. I've been talking to various people and I have decided to section you indefinitely.'

Rodney broke down in tears. A female nurse patted him on the back looking concerned, as she had not heard of anything so harsh in all of the eleven years at her job.

'Why me?' spluttered Rodney.

'I'm sorry, but it's for the best,' said Doctor Wright. There was a pregnant pause and then, when Rodney had perked up she said, 'A series of injections are going to be administered to you on a weekly basis starting from next week. Have you got any objections to this?'

'No.'

'Good. That will be all,' said the rather gaunt looking Doctor Wright.

Her expression never changed all of the time that she saw Rodney. The other nurses picked up on this and were discussing the severity of the sentence. 'He's obviously off his head, but that was tough,' said the male nurse, out of earshot of Rodney.

They escorted him back to the dormitory. 'Keep a good eye on him,' said the female nurse to the male nurse. Rodney spotted a newspaper as he walked through the smoke room. Again, no one was about so he proceeded to read the national newspaper headlines. He noted that the paper was two days old. He sat down, exasperated.

"*MAN KILLS SEVEN*" said the headline.

A man from Leamington Spa has killed seven people, including two police officers. Many were injured during mad driving events. Rodney Pendleton is now in Rampton Mental Hospital where he is being analysed around the clock. 'It is not known what triggered this off,' said a doctor at the hospital. Police are looking into an incident that took place in a Leamington Spa book shop, where Rodney was seen leaving the burning shop which is now completely gutted. A priest, who wishes to remain anonymous, said that Rodney had approached him for help soon after the blaze occurred, only to suggest that he see the police.

Then, a photograph of Rodney that was taken some years ago and was quite flattering, was there in full colour for the world to see.

Rodney was disturbed by a nurse who knew his case rather well. She immediately took the paper from him in an authoritative manner. 'You shouldn't be reading this. Put it all behind you and start afresh,' were her words.

'But please, I need to read what's been said,' Rodney asserted.

'No.' She walked away as he was pleading.

'They're a tough lot here,' said a friendly man, a plump, balding, grey-haired chap with pure blue eyes. His eyebrows met in the middle. He seems friendly enough though, thought Rodney.

'How long have you been here?' enquired Rodney.

'Two years, but I don't know how long I have got to go.'

Feeling very depressed now, Rodney got up and said, 'See you later.' But that was the last he saw of him.

Chapter 5

Rodney lay in his bed. Sharon appeared from round the corner. 'Oh hi, you're awake now I see.'

Rodney was overjoyed to see a friendly face. 'Hi, how are you?'

'Shocked at what you have done.' There was a pause. 'You've changed Rodders, you're not the same, but I am still pleased to see you, it's weird.'

'Sit down please.'

She had a suitcase that she immediately opened. It had an electric shaver, shoes, shirts and all manner of things. 'You're all over the TV and newspapers, the radio, everything. The press have been hounding me.'

'I know, I saw it in the papers. Can you get me newspaper cuttings please?'

'Yes, of course I can. I bought loads, it's weird,' she repeated again.

He whispered into her ear, 'You've got to get me out of here. I have looked at the windows and with an Allen key of the right size, I can be out of here.'

Sharon looked shocked. Knowing how mad he had become, she thought that she should go along with him, but not actually take action. I've got to tell the staff, she thought. 'Okay, yes,' she said.

'Great. Bring it with you tomorrow.'

'Okay,' she said. 'I've brought you some of your favourite things,' Sharon said as she was emptying the suitcase.

'That's an interesting suitcase,' Rodney said.

'It's a Rollator. It can go up and down stairs and over kerbs, it's amazing.'

'Only the best for me, eh? How's our son doing and where is he?'

'Oh, he's at his gran's. I thought it would be too much for him.' Then Rodney became low again. Sharon noticed this. 'Cheer up, cheer up!'

Rodney replied sarcastically, 'I've been told that I am in here indefinitely.'

'Oh, I didn't realise that.'

'I'm also on a series of weekly injections.'

'Oh.' Again there was a pause. 'I can't stop long,' said a tired looking Sharon. They kissed one another tenderly. 'I know you, I know you well and I know that this isn't like you. You're a good man, the salt of the earth. You have not got a bad bone in your body. You've got a good heart and I must tell this to the staff here, because you should not be here.' Sharon then wept uncontrollably as Rodney held her in his arms.

'Some things happened, Sharon, that I can't explain. I wish I could.'

A staff member looked in, concerned by the wailing of Sharon. 'She's okay,' Rodney said calmly.

That night, Rodney was having a bath when suddenly, he had an idea. When there was no one looking, he could smash the glass with the metal seat and escape. He quickly dried himself and got his clothes on. He took one almighty swing into the centre of the glass, just as a nurse was saying to another nurse, 'His wife says that he wants an Allen key so that he can escape through the glass.' Just as she said the word "glass", there was a terrific sound of smashed glass that could be heard all over the hospital. 'What the hell was that?' said the nurse.

All of the staff darted everywhere, except the area that had actually been broken. No one knew exactly where the noise had come from. Rodney was soon over the high security fence. He was still agile. He tore along alleyways and over gardens.

At the same time, the head nurse was on the phone to the police. 'Hello, there has been a breakout from Rampton Hospital. We don't know as yet who it is, but we'll soon be able to tell you,' the nurse was embarrassed to say.

'Okay, we'll be on to it right away,' came the gruff voice.

A nurse found the bathroom window broken. The speed of Rodney's disappearance was phenomenal. Falling into a pond from a great height didn't deter Rodney, he just kept on moving. A big beam of light fell on Rodney momentarily. It was a police helicopter, its light swaying to and fro, not stopping on anything in particular. It was going away from where Rodney was heading.

An angry dog barked as it pounced on Rodney. He kicked at it wildly as the dog bit him in the calf. A high kick to the dog's face made it even more fierce. Rodney managed to go over a fence before the dog had a chance to hold onto him. The dog's whimpers from its damaged head alerted the owners. A man and a woman saw Rodney's feet as they went over the fence. Seeing the police helicopter, they both thought at the same time that it was an escape from Rampton. Soon the man was on the telephone to the police. 'Hello, we have just had a man attack our dog. We saw him go over our garden fence, heading away from the hospital.'

'Thank you, we are on to it now.' The phone call was abruptly aborted by the policeman.

The phone in the station rang again. This time it was the head nurse of the hospital. 'Hello, this is Rampton again. Our worst case scenario has occurred, Rodney Pendleton is at large.'

'Thank you,' said the police officer. Putting down the phone he said, 'Right, get every man available from all ranks, this is a red alert. A man who is highly dangerous is on the loose.'

Rodney ran across a busy road, narrowly missing getting run over. He thought that maybe it would have been better if he had been run over by that lorry. He stopped for breath at the roadside. He analysed his wound. The dog had done a lot of damage. Pulling his leg away had made it a lot worse, but he knew that if he hadn't, he would probably still be there now and caught. Right, thought Rodney, the next lorry that comes my way, I am going to end it all. It's this, or prison for the remainder of my life. A gigantic lorry hurtled towards him. He stood at the side of the road, and when the time was right, he jumped so that his head would be crushed. But the lorry driver was alert and swerved. One wheel caught Rodney's foot slightly.

The driver got out immediately. Rodney didn't know whether to be relieved or sad. 'Why do you want to kill yourself mate? It can't be all that bad, can it?' the driver said whilst pulling Rodney out from beneath the lorry. Suddenly, Rodney had an idea. He banged the driver's head against the side of the lorry, then pounced into the cab, feeling the pain from the dog bite and the lorry injury. He turned the ignition on and proceeded as fast as he could into the path of other vehicles. The man was now on his feet and shaking his fists at Rodney as the lorry went out of his sight. Rodney was now thinking that he could not have planned this any better. The fuel gauge read full. It was a relatively new lorry and he could tell from the way it was handling that it was empty. The speedometer read eighty. It seemed that it would go a lot faster, but Rodney didn't want to make it obvious that he was on the run. Heading up north he thought that he would be safer in the wilderness. He looked to his left and saw a Karfriend full of goodies — sandwiches, a flask of tea, biscuits, chocolate bars, as well as a wallet, camera and many other things, some that could come in useful, especially the mobile phone. He could ring up Sharon and put her mind at rest.

A motorway service station was nearby. Can I risk it? he thought. I have got to go to the toilet. So into the service station he went.

Meanwhile, the lorry driver, whose name was Michael Donovan, was flagging down a police car. The police pulled up. Blood was streaming down Michael's head. 'Can you please help me? A man has got my lorry.'

'Get in.'

Michael got into the back of the car. A policewoman reached into the glove box and produced a pack of handkerchiefs. As she was giving them to Michael, the driver said, 'What is your registration number?' Michael told them. 'Okay, what did he look like?'

'I didn't have a chance to notice. All I can say is that he was tall.'

'What happened?'

'He jumped out in front of me. I'm sure that he was trying to kill himself. I-I-I- swerved,' he stammered. 'If I hadn't swerved he would have killed himself.'

'Okay, calm down. We'll get you to a hospital. If you see the lorry, give us a shout. Relax now. Just tell us the name of the company that's on the lorry and is there anything in it?'

'No,' said Michael, telling them that the name was "Fur Longleys".

Rodney tried to ring Sharon on the mobile phone, but there was no answer. He tried again, but still no reply. Sharon was having a shower and didn't hear the phone. Rodney chucked the phone into the Karfriend in disgust. Soon he was on the Scottish border. The speedometer rarely went below sixty. He knew that he could not afford to be stopped. He saw a police car on the other side of the motorway

The police car had spotted him. The policeman said, 'The Fur Longleys' lorry has been seen heading northwards at junction 10 on the M74 near Lesmahagow, over.'

Meanwhile, Rodney had decided he had to get off the motorway in case he had been spotted. He took the B7086 and ahead he saw a secluded lay-by. By this time he was exhausted, so he pulled into the lay-by. He was relieved to see that there was a bed in the cabin. He climbed into it, drew the curtains across and was soon fast asleep.

He was awakened by the sound of heavy rain against the windows of the lorry. He got up slowly and gingerly drew back the curtains. He immediately noticed a breakfast van opposite. He thought that this would be the very best place to hide away from the police. He looked at his watch and saw that it was ten in the morning. Suddenly, he thought why not look at the coin holder in the lorry? To his surprise there was £24 in notes and coins. He took a note and decided to go and get himself some food from the van. Closing the door, he made sure that the lorry was locked. Slowly walking to the van, Rodney looked around. It was a very busy lay-by. At the van there was a man in his early thirties and a girl of about seventeen. The girl was lively, she had blonde hair and was heavily made-up. 'Hello,' she said in a Scottish accent.

'Hi ya,' Rodney replied. There was a long pause. 'Can I have two bacon sandwiches, please,' said a polite Rodney.

'You may,' replied the girl. She giggled, finding Rodney rather attractive. She was too and certainly didn't need all of the make-up. The man behind the counter looked at Rodney and knew that he had seen him somewhere before. 'There you are laddie,' she joked.

'Ta,' said Rodney, laughing at the cheeky girl and gave her a broad smile. He walked away still grinning.

The rain had stopped now. He was thinking that perhaps he should have got a drink, as the two flasks in the lorry were running low. He struggled for the right key, but finally found it. A man walked by and got into his lorry, a fat man with a beard. He looked at Rodney and smiled. Rodney smiled back. Soon Rodney was eating the bacon sandwiches. They were good — smothered in a rich butter and crispy rind which Rodney appreciated. He opened the flask and poured a cupful of tea. Again he thought how lucky he was to be in such a favourable hideaway. Unfortunately for him, it was to be short-lived.

A lorry pulled up. The man in it opened up the paper and saw Fur Longleys written into the article. He read the whole story and immediately got onto the police on his mobile phone. 'Hello, that man that you are chasing in a Fur Langleys' lorry is in a lay-by on the B7086 heading west.'

'Thank you,' said the policeman.

The lorry driver was inquisitive and got out of his vehicle. He was a thin man with a beer belly, heavy eyebrows and mysterious eyes. The rather scruffy man walked past Rodney's lorry and then turned again sharply, looking directly at him. Rodney was quick to hide his face. He stooped down but not soon enough. The lorry driver got a good look at him. That's the man, thought the lorry driver and quickly got into his cab, knowing that he too could be in danger.

Meanwhile, the police were on their way. Rodney was just finishing his breakfast and was thinking that the man was just a little bit suspicious. He was sipping his tea when a screech of tyres was heard. Rodney's worst thoughts had come to fruition.

He could see that there was a police car at the other end as well through the mirror. He quickly opened the cab door and jumped over a barbed wire fence. This left Rodney cascading down a steep hill, hitting rocks as he went. Within seconds he was out of sight of the police, who were scratching their heads in dismay. Still Rodney was rolling away to safety. He was getting more bruised by the second. Suddenly, he stopped rolling. He had hit a well. Rodney gave out a large groan. At that exact time a young woman was putting out the washing onto a line. She heard the groan and walked towards the well. This was a long distance as the garden was extensive. She strolled the two acres, but just as she was about to discover Rodney, she heard her son shout out that the police were at the door. She ran, her long blonde hair flowing in the wind. She was a fit thirty and was visually stunning. She wondered what the police could want. This was such a quiet cottage.

'The police are at the door,' repeated her son.

'Hello,' she said.

'Sorry to trouble you. A dangerous man is on the loose and we have reason to believe that he could be in this vicinity.' Just as he said this, Rodney became more alert.

'I have just heard a voice groaning in my back garden I think.'

'Right, send for backup,' said the policeman to the policewoman. Then he walked cautiously around the side of the building into the rear garden. 'Whereabouts did the noise come from?' he asked kindly.

'Over there.' She pointed over to the corner of the garden.

'We had better wait for backup,' he said, stopping and making sure that the policewoman took notice of what he had said.

'They're on their way,' she said to the policeman.

He frowned as he looked around. He was a handsome man with a pronounced moustache. The policewoman was small, but cute. She had mousey hair and a beauty spot on her chin. She was twenty-two but only looked sixteen. Her name was Wendy. They walked gingerly towards the well. Rodney had clocked them. A chance to escape, he thought as he manoeuvred away from the well and along the hedge up the next-door neighbour's garden. They were still only halfway up the garden when Rodney was walking up to the front of the next door neighbour's house. He stood upright. A police car was about to turn the corner onto the road that Rodney was crossing. He had literally just gone out of sight up an alleyway when the car screeched around the corner. He could just make out the faint sound of the police radio mentioning his name. He soon made himself scarce. There was a maze of alleyways and he thought to himself that somebody somewhere was looking after him. If there was a place to escape from the police, this was it.

Nothing was said as the police wandered silently up the garden, which was immaculate with all manner of plants.

Sharon heard the news on her car radio. 'Rodney Pendleton has escaped from Rampton Mental Hospital'.

By this time Rodney was well away. Suddenly, in front of him was a fence with a steep slope leading to an electric railway line. He was seriously thinking to himself, not another railway line, and also had the thought of doing himself in again. By now he was far away from any housing. He had made great time by running. He was far from any police. He looked for an opening in the fence and again he was lucky. Sure enough, there was a slit in the fence. He pulled it up and tried to get through. It was not big enough, so using his hands he clawed away at the soil. This time he nearly got through. He tried moving some more soil and this time was successful. 'Phew!' He inhaled deeply. By this time he was sweating badly. This is it, he mused, what have I got to live for now? I've got no chance of getting away from the police and I have a life in a mental institution injected with drugs for life! He felt tired now and at his lowest ebb in his entire life. He waited for a train to come. He did not have to wait for long. From his side came a train at one hundred miles per hour. Rodney noticed it from a long way off, as it was on a very straight track. He lay across the track. Facing the train he counted down the expected crunch time. 'Ten, nine, eight, seven, six, FIVE, FOUR, THREE, TWO...' Rodney had not got the bottle. He quickly moved his body so that he was parallel to the rails. He kept as close to the ground as possible, as the frightening body of the train sped past.

Suddenly, he sensed a voice in his head saying calmly, 'YOU ARE SAVED — YOU ARE CHOSEN.' Rodney did not know what to make of the sound in his head. He scrambled up the steep embankment. He looked for a hole in the fence, but was unsuccessful. This time he climbed up the fence, catching the same leg again on the barbed wire at the top. After he had jumped down, he analysed his leg again. It was in a poor state. He knew that he needed treatment for it. He was pondering whether or not to go into one of the houses that he could see on the horizon. He came to a river and thought that the last thing that his leg needed was a dousing in a filthy river, so he walked along the river side. He gained extra energy from somewhere and soon walked at a quicker pace. Suddenly, he found a bridge. To get to it, he had to pass a fisherman. Rodney looked scruffy at best, so to avoid confrontation, he walked broadly round him. He clambered across the bridge and walked through a field that had all sorts of things in it. Rodney thought to himself that the farmer must be neglectful. Soon he was wading through stinging nettles heading towards a farmhouse.

Sharon was on the phone to Rampton Hospital. 'Have they found Rodney?' she blurted.

'Sorry, what ward do you want or doctor?'

'Doctor Wright,' came the distraught reply.

'Putting you through.'

'Hello, Doctor Wright, this is Sharon, Rodney's wife.'

'Oh hello.'

'Is he there yet?' asked a worried Sharon.

'Sorry, he is still on the loose in Scotland I believe, but the police are doing all they can to catch him.'

'Okay, okay.' And with that, Sharon put the phone down without a thank you. She was stunned.

Rodney walked into the farmhouse. He was past caring. He wandered through the lounge and up the stairs. No one was about. He found the bathroom and in a cabinet was a first aid kit. Rodney looked at himself in the mirror. Looking a state, he decided to wash and then he dragged his comb through his hair. He cleaned his wounds. It was not a pretty picture. Rodney had done a first aid course in the past and he made a good job of his wounds. He gave out a yelp as he patted surgical spirit onto the wound with a cotton wool swab. Then there was a noise from upstairs. Rodney quickly bandaged up his leg. He shut the door so that just a slight gap was showing. A woman appeared. She walked down the stairs singing to herself. Rodney gave out an audible sigh. Slowly and silently he walked down the stairs. They creaked. There was a door at the base of the hall that led to the outside. He slowly turned the handle and at that moment the woman screamed loudly. Rodney opened the door and ran as fast as she could. The woman screamed louder still, running after Rodney half-heartedly. Her husband came out of a shed and ran after Rodney. Rodney had little time to look behind. He had never run as fast in his life. He was by now in a small forest. The farmer, a red faced man in a straw hat, ran as fast as he could, but being sixty-five could not keep up very well. Rodney was gradually getting deeper and deeper into a bog. The farmer had chosen a different route and soon was up to his knees in mud. Rodney somehow got out gradually. He felt that he needed to help the farmer out. His wife stood at the edge of the bog urging her husband back out towards her. Rodney thought that if he were to help the farmer out, he would then have a more fruitful stay at Rampton Hospital. Soon this thought went and he headed away from the river and away from bog land. He looked into the distance and could see the farmer's wife placing a large branch towards her husband, who seemed to be sinking deeper still.

Soon Rodney was out of sight of any houses. He climbed over a fence and caught sight of a bench at the river's edge in the distance. By this time Rodney was in need of a rest and headed for the seat. Slowly, he dragged himself across a muddy, rain-soaked field. Rodney paced himself. He thought that as long as he kept up the speed that he was going, he would make it to the bench in five minutes.

Soon he was at the bench. He gave out another sigh as he sat down. Rodney felt in his pocket and found the mobile phone. Time I let Sharon know where I am and that I am okay, he thought. He tapped in the correct number for his wife, noticing that he had plenty of battery power and a good signal.

'Hello,' said Sharon.

'Hello, it's me, Rodney.'

'Oh, thank God, are you OK?'

'Yes, I'm fine. Are you?'

'Yes, I've been worried sick.'

'I'm fine,' he repeated.

'Where are you?'

'In Scotland somewhere.' Rodney looked and could just see a road with a sign on and just in view, a little village. He got up and walked as fast as he could over a bridge as he was talking. 'I'm just walking over a river. I can see a sign. The village is Sandford, but you must not divulge that to anyone.'

'I'm on my way. I am coming to get you. I promise I won't tell a soul.'

'Are you sure?'

'Yes.'

'It will take you three hours at least!'

'That's okay. Is there anything you need?'

'No, just you. You're a star.'

'Bye.'

'Bye.'

Sharon gathered a map, torch, and everything else she could think of that would be of some use. She got into her car and was away to Scotland.

Rodney was thinking about the voice that he had heard just after the train had gone past. 'You are saved, you are chosen.'

What did it mean? Who was it? Rodney lay down on a dry bit of grass. 'It was me, your God, Jesus.' Rodney got up quickly and looked around. There was no one about at all. 'YOU ARE THE CHOSEN ONE,' came the voice again. Rodney thought that he was going mad. He looked over the hedgerow. No one was to be seen.

Meanwhile, the farmer had managed to get out using his wife's long stick. 'Quick, let's get on the phone,' he said in a broad Scottish accent, shaking his legs to get rid of the excess mud. 'He was in our house? Let's find out if he stole anything.'

'I told you we should get a dog,' she moaned.

'Oh never mind that, woman, let's get onto the police.'

They wandered silently back into the farmhouse. He took off his boots and got onto the phone. He punched in the numbers with his muddy fingers. 'Hello, Sandford police? Hello, we're from Little Rock farmhouse. We have had a burglary.'

'Was it a man?'

'Yes.'

'Right, we'll be round within the next ten minutes.'

'Okay, thanks.'

Rodney was still spooked by the voices. He looked at his watch for the first time in ages. Two o'clock it said. The sun was high in the sky, so he had guessed that it was something of that nature. A large lorry went past, the first vehicle to do so since he had lain down. I can't go to sleep, he thought, I've got to stay awake for Sharon. Then he began to think, what a good wife I have in Sharon. She is a star. He then began thinking about other relatives and friends who had wives that were not a patch on Sharon. She was immaculate in every way, so understanding.

At the same time Sharon was wondering how she could protect him. She had the brains to put their passports into the bag that she had with her. She also pondered about where the nearest airport could be. She pulled into a garage to put some diesel in. I'll put the satellite navigation on in a moment, she thought. She proceeded to fill the tank up as far as she could. There was a long queue and she thought, I hope Rodney doesn't telephone me now!

A police car entered the long lane which led on to Little Rock farm. The car skidded to a halt. 'Where did the man head for?' asked the policeman abruptly.

'He went in that direction,' said the farmer. 'He took a load of first aid and went.'

'Thank you,' said the policeman.

Suddenly, there were three police cars screeching to a halt on the farmhouse's gravel drive.

'This must be an escaped convict or something,' said the farmer to his wife.

The police continued to question the farmer about how long ago it was, while the other police went on foot. Police dogs were being let out of vans at the farmhouse to help the police find Rodney. They searched everywhere.

Sharon was on her way, using satellite navigation and her foot hard on the accelerator. She was making good time. The navigation system said that the estimated time of arrival was four o'clock, but would this be in time for Rodney? He seemed like a sitting duck at the moment.

Rodney thought again about the farmer and how soon he could inform the police. Then he had the idea of going back and walking along the river for a bit and then returning by a different route. My damaged leg will suffer, but it's my only option. They could have dogs! he thought. I can't keep moving away from my position, it would not be fair on Sharon. He walked over to the river and thought that he had heard police dogs and realised that he had been thinking that subconsciously. The faint noise of police dogs was getting louder by the minute. He was wondering why the police don't train the dogs to be a little quieter. He quickly walked a good way up the river. He came out a few times at different stages, making for the trees, then he went back to the river and walked to near the sign where he would meet Sharon.

By this time, Sharon was leaving the motorway.

Rodney's leg was hurting badly. He could now see the police in the distance. Time to do some tree climbing, he thought. Luckily, there was a tree that was easy to climb. He soon reached the top. By now the dogs were near to the river. His leg was aching so much that he thought of taking off the bandage. His scheme was working, the dogs were going in the wrong direction. But time was desperately running out. He looked at his watch. It was 4.28 p.m. He had made himself so comfortable up the tree that he was drifting off. No, he thought, I could easily fall off! Keep with it. He was in need of sleep, but had to hold in there. The dogs were getting closer. Suddenly, a car pulled up near to the sign. It was Sharon. Rodney was so fast getting down the tree that he nearly hurt himself. He dropped down, in full view of the police.

'Get him boy,' shouted a copper.

A group of dogs came running at Rodney. He limped over a fence and just as a dog was about to bite him, he got into the car.

'Go, go, go!' shouted Rodney.

The police were soon to report the situation to their colleagues.

'Don't go so fast,' said Rodney. 'We don't want it obvious that we're on the run. They didn't get a good look at the. car, I made sure of that. You made good time, didn't you?'

'Yes, I broke a few speed limits,' laughed Sharon. 'I couldn't see you in that place all your life.'

'It's much appreciated, I can assure you.'

'Right, what's the plan then?'

'We go to Jersey. I know that there are a lot of flights out there from Glasgow.'

'Okay, okay.'

A broad smile came on Rodney's face as he looked at Sharon and she smiled back. 'Can we stop off at a Little Chef or something?'

'Yes, sure.'

They pulled into a roadside cafe. 'I'll bring you something out because you're a bit notorious.'

'Okay,' said a sad Rodney. He did not like the idea that he was so conspicuous. What can I do? he thought to himself. How can I disguise myself? I can't, I've got to get through on my passport. Perhaps quickness is the key? Will the police be at the airport? They're bound to be!

Sharon returned to the car. 'That's your tea,' she said with a grin.

'That was quick,' he said. As he was tucking into the fish and chips he said, 'We can't go to the airport, love, the police will be all over the place!'

'Okay, what do you suggest?'

'Glen Coe.' There was a pause. 'There are lots of good bed and breakfast places there.'

'Why not just sleep in the car?'

'Well, I was thinking of you.'

'Let's play it by ear. Head for Inverness anyway. The further up north the better, I say.'

'Okay then,' said a tired Sharon.

'You need to get some sleep.'

'Yes.'

As soon as he had eaten the food, Rodney gradually fell asleep. Sharon drove on to Inverness.

She journeyed as far as she thought safe. She parked the car in a lay-by near to Fort William. Soon, she too was asleep. The car was parked discreetly away from the main road.

The police had guessed that Sharon was the instigator of Rodney's escape. 'Yes, she's in a black and silver Ford Focus, last seen in Sandford, over.' The police were pointing at the map of Scotland, not really knowing where to look.

The morning came and Rodney was the first to stir. He poured a cup of coffee for himself from the flask that Sharon had thoughtfully brought. Curious, Rodney put the radio on low volume, to hear the eight o'clock news. 'The fugitive, Rodney Pendleton, has now been on the loose for two consecutive days. It is feared he may be abroad or in the highlands of Scotland. Police have asked the public to be vigilant,' came the report. At least they haven't given out the registration number, thought Rodney.

Sharon awoke. 'What was that I heard on the radio?'

'Oh, a fugitive in Scotland and please be vigilant,' said Rodney. 'Perhaps we can stay in Scotland for a few days and then go to Jersey.'

'Okay, whatever,' said a sad Sharon. 'Don't I get a cup of tea then?'

'No, you can have a cup of coffee though,' laughed Rodney, trying to make light of the situation. 'Ooh, my leg's killing me.'

'Why didn't you say earlier? I have a first aid kit in the back of the car.'

'Oh, good.'

Sharon reached out onto the parcel shelf and lifted the lid. 'There you are, sir,' she smiled.

Rodney was in no mood for smiling. His leg revealed a complete mess. Again he removed what was a mixture of all manner of things found mainly in rivers. He dabbed again with surgical spirit. 'Ouch!' he said.

Sharon said, 'Don't be such a baby!' She laughed again. Then she looked more closely and thought that this was probably a job for a fully qualified nurse, but she kept quiet.

'I'll do the driving if you like,' said a solemn Rodney as he finished off bandaging himself.

'Okay,' said Sharon.

The door creaked as Rodney opened it. The fresh air hit him hard. A camper van was parked very close and Rodney struggled to get past. He got into the driver's seat and immediately started the car.

'What's the rush?' said Sharon.

'I don't know. I've got the strangest feeling about this place. I feel uneasy, okay? I have had some strange things happen to me just recently. I tried to kill myself,' he said whilst driving onto the main road. 'I tried to do myself in on a railway line and just as I was going to finish myself off, my body sort of moved itself off the line and a voice from nowhere said, "you are saved, you are the chosen one". Don't ask me to explain because I can't.'

'Do you believe that it was the voice of God?'

'Yes, yes, I do because it said later that it was the voice of Jesus.'

'I believe in God. Do you?'

'I do now.'

'Good. Great.' There was a long pause. 'Do you realise that now you're a born again Christian, as such you are guaranteed a place in Heaven?'

'Oh, don't go all Christian on me now, please.'

'Okay, I won't say another word,' said Sharon politely.

Shortly after their car had pulled away, a police car drove into the lay-by they had just left.

'Did you see that?' exclaimed Rodney.

'What?' said Sharon.

'A police car just entered that car park! Quick, we'll leave this road as soon as we can.'

'Don't worry,' said Sharon

Sure enough, there was a small road that led to a steep incline. They drove to the top. 'Right, now we're here, what do we do now?'

'I don't know,' said a timid Sharon.

'Starve to death?' said Rodney in a fierce voice.

Suddenly, a red mist engulfed their car. 'THE DEVIL IS AT HAND,' said a loud voice.

Rodney looked at Sharon. 'You didn't just say anything, did you?'

'No.'

'Did you just say, "the devil is as hand"?

'No,' replied Rodney.

They were in the wilderness. There was nothing about. But little did they know they were in the thick of it. The red mist was now very thick. They could not see a thing outside.

Immediately, a horned creature was visible with a long tongue, a gigantic tail and totally red. 'It's the Devil!' screamed Sharon. 'It's Satan.' Rodney jumped out of the car. 'No,' screamed Sharon.

'You were the chosen one, but I have outwitted your God, I always win,' said the Devil.

'DO NOT LISTEN TO THE DEVIL, HE IS THE PRINCE OF ALL LIARS,' came a thunderous voice.

'I have beaten the man you call God. There is no escape from me. You are not the chosen one. Your God has lied again.'

Sharon tried to start the car, but it would not. She opened the car door and ran around to hold Rodney. Holding him tightly she shouted, 'Go away!'

The Devil just laughed. Now the Devil was laughing non-stop. 'Come on, let's go,' said Rodney.

'What? Just like that? I don't think so,' said Lucifer, his tail sweeping them both off their feet.

'Let's go. Run!' said Sharon.

'You were God's perfect couple, but I am to change that,' said the Devil. They tried to escape but the Devil's tail kept them off their balance.

'Pray, pray your way out of it, Rodney,' pleaded Sharon.

'Our Father who art in heaven, hallowed be thy name, thy kingdom come... I can't remember the rest of it,' shouted Rodney.

'I can't either.'

'Oh, what a pity,' said Satan sarcastically. 'Why do you pray to your God when you already know that you are my prey, huh, huh?'

'There is only one winner and that is Jesus, you fool,' said Sharon.

'Watch your tongue, little one.' And with that, the Devil swiped Sharon off her feet and dashed her against a rock, which was just visible enough for Rodney to see.

'Can't you do anything?' asked Rodney of God. There was no reply. 'You coward,' shouted Rodney at the Devil. 'Can't you pick on a man?'

'You foolish man. How dare you toy with me. Take that.' Rodney was being dragged and beaten by the Devil's tail. 'And that.' Fire scorched his already damaged leg from the Devil's breath. 'Where is your God to save you now? Where is your God?' repeated Lucifer.

'Rodney, Rodney, are you all right?' Sharon cuddled Rodney.

He lay on the ground. 'I'm all right. It's me he wants. Go away, it's me that he needs. Honestly.'

Sharon said, 'I'll never let you go, Rodney. Whichever realm that you go to, I will go too.'

'I think I'm going to cry,' said Satan. 'Away with you, you blubbering creature.' Again the Devil's tail struck Sharon, only this time Rodney holds onto it. He was flung in the same direction. Rodney bit the Devil's tail hard. 'Ooch,' said the Devil. 'Got me again. What a pity you have no God to save you.' Then suddenly, Satan unleashed his tongue. It swept Rodney off his feet.

'Whatever you do, you can't damn me,' said Rodney. The Devil wrapped his tongue around Rodney's neck. Rodney gasped for breath. 'You can't damn me,' Rodney repeatedly croaked.

'Bollocks,' asserted Lucifer. And with that he pulled away, thus strangling Rodney with his tongue until Rodney was still. His eyes were static and wide open. 'Ha, ha, ha.' The madman danced up and down as if his feet were on something hot. He laughed crazily. Beelzebub disappeared.

Sharon ran up to Rodney. 'Rodney, Rodney.' She looked down upon him, stroking his cheeks. 'Please come back to life, please.'

Then the voice of the Devil hissed, 'HE'S IN HELL NOW.'

'No! Oh no, please.' Sharon wept a lot. Her tears poured

rapidly onto Rodney's forehead and eyes which were still wide open. Her tears streamed, overflowing with love. She tenderly felt his heart. Thud, thud, then no more. Sharon collapsed onto Rodney.

Unbeknownst to Sharon, a white, swirling, cool, clean sensation encapsulated Rodney. Suddenly he was in HEAVEN, with angels all around him. Softly, a voice said authoritatively, 'Your wife's tears saved you, something more precious than holy water anointed your head.'

THE END